# THE AUTHOR

Michael O'Donovan ('Frank O'Connor') was born in Cork in 1903. As a young man he fought on the Republican side during the Irish Civil War, being captured by Free State soldiers in February 1923, and spending almost a year in an internment camp.

From 1924 to 1938 he worked as a librarian, an occupation which allowed him the time and opportunity to educate himself (his family had been too poor to send him to university) and to develop as a writer. Many of his early stories were accepted for publication in the *Irish Statesman* by 'AE' (George Russell), who regarded him as the most promising young Irish writer since James Stephens. As his literary reputation grew, he came to the attention of W.B. Yeats, who said of him that he was 'doing for Ireland what Chekhov did for Russia'. Thanks to Yeats' influence, O'Connor became a director of the famous Abbey Theatre in 1935.

In 1940 O'Connor was a co-founder, with Séan O'Faoláin and others, of the magazine *The Bell*. He also gave talks on current events and the theatre for the BBC, and from 1943 to 1945 he wrote a series of weekly articles for the *Sunday Independent* under the name of 'Ben Mayo'.

O'Connor's writings were particularly highly regarded in America, and in 1952 and 1953 he lectured on Irish literature and conducted seminars on creative writing at Northwestern University and Harvard. In 1953 he married a young American, Harriet Rice (his first marriage, to Evelyn Bowen had ended in 1949). They were to live in America until 1961. By then O'Connor's health was failing, and he had become increasingly homesick for his native country. His last five years were spent in Dublin, his reputation secure as one of the greatest Irish writers of his time. He died in March 1966.

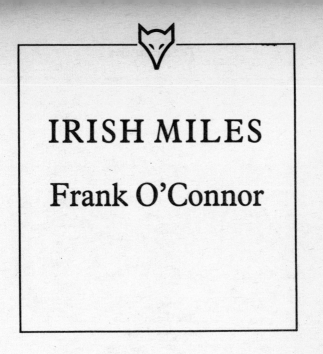

# IRISH MILES

## Frank O'Connor

*New Introduction by*
*Brendan Kennelly*

**THE HOGARTH PRESS**

LONDON

To Stan Stewart

Published in 1988 by
The Hogarth Press
30 Bedford Square, London WCIB 3RP

First published in Great Britain by Macmillan & Co. Ltd 1947
Copyright © Frank O'Connor 1947
Introduction copyright © Brendan Kennelly 1988

British Library Cataloguing in Publication Data

O'Connor, Frank
Irish miles.
1. Ireland – Description and travel –
1901 – 1950
Rn: Michael Francis O'Donovan    I. Title
914.15'04822    DA977

ISBN 0 7012 0786 8

Printed in Great Britain by
Cox & Wyman Ltd,
Reading, Berkshire

# INTRODUCTION

Imagine a man who is inspired by a passion for this country's past, expressed in its architecture, archaeology, history and literature. Many, though by no means all, of his fellow countrymen are not only ignorant of the treasures of their heritage but are at best indifferent to, and at worst approving of, its neglect and destruction. This man is in love with the evidence of the past and though painfully conscious of the prevailing lack of concern decides to see it with his own eyes, and in the company of kindred spirits. The country is Ireland, the man is Frank O'Connor: his friends have colourful names, hungry minds and enthusiastic hearts. Together they form a band of explorers and adventurers mounted on (mostly) reliable bicycles and equipped with enough curiosity and energy to propel them all over Ireland in search of the thrilling remains of a lost civilisation. The result is *Irish Miles*, the fascinating chronicle of that quest. The book is history, autobiography, social commentary, drama, travel-writing of an especially gripping kind, shot through with the critical wit and bitter-sweet comedy of which O'Connor was a master. The past is Ireland's most complex reality. Today's 'Northern Troubles' are directly traceable to it. Some Irish people live, it would seem, almost completely for the past: there is a vast popular culture of songs, stories and poems in which a glamourised history is seen as the repository of heroism, lost focus of inspiration, and radiant alternative to contemporary drabness. It comes to seem more vital and important than the present. When I say that some people live *for* the past, I mean precisely that. It is generally taken for granted in Western European culture that people live and work to try to make the present more enjoyable and civilised with the aim, unspoken, perhaps, but ever-present, of moulding the future into a more tolerable place for the young and unborn. In Ireland, you could be forgiven for thinking that many people live for the sake of the distinguished dead, out of a sense of responsibility towards the exhorations of those ferociously articulate ghosts who, nicely detached in eternity, must be chuckling at the solemn respect paid to them.

'I am not sure that any country can afford to discard what I have called "the backward look", but we in Ireland can afford it less than any other because without it we have nothing and are nothing.' These words of Frank O'Connor conclude his study of Irish literature in *The Backward Look*. The past is a proud possession. The past is spiritual wealth. The past is identity ('without it we are nothing'). The past is the only hope we have of making sense of this dull, pointless, shapeless, ugly, blinkered, besotted, greedy present.

That is the logic of O'Connor's thinking. Is it Romantic? Out of touch? For all I know, it may well be both these damning things when seen in the light of another life, another country, another culture. In the light of Irish life and Irish culture, however, it is a sane, shrewd, canny approach, a clear path through a confused jungle. If, in Ireland, you pay intelligent attention to the past you are no likely to be deluded by the complexities of the present. But it is a question of balance. An uncritical, adulatory pondering of the past can lead to sentimental or even murderous oversimplifications of history and its reverberating consequences (at one level, *Irish Miles* is a severely critical study of these same consequences). What is needed in a truly creative approach is a capacity for detached scrutiny; a proper, and therefore rare, respect; an unfailing sense of humour; an ability to enter into animated conversation with either the living or the dead, or both simultaneously, at the drop of a hat or the rattle of a skeleton; a blend of scholarship and speculation; an ability to personalise every abstraction but more especially every *place* in Ireland; a calm appreciation of the casual lunacies that are the backbone of Irish life. Without this humorous detachment, a writer contemplating that vast past would soon be a know-all bore or a garrulous crank. Fortunately, Frank O'Connor is one of

Ireland's wittiest, most penetrating writers; and laughter is never far from his lips. His study of Ireland's past, in literature, archaeology and architecture, is blessedly free from erudite heaviness; O'Connor *knows* a lot, and he imparts his knowledge with a light, graceful touch. His prose is a delight, charming, impish, informative. In *Irish Miles* he takes his readers on one of the most pleasant, funny and revealing journeys they are ever likely to go on.

*Irish Miles* is rare in Irish travel literature for many reasons. One important reason is that O'Connor's preoccupation with the past was so constant and deep. I have already referred to *The Backward Look*, the most refreshing personal assessment to date of Irish literature and the forces that produced it. As well as that, O'Connor is a gifted translator of Irish poetry. His collections, *Kings, Lords and Commons* and *The Little Monasteries* are pure joy for their music, clarity and inspired lightness. O'Connor translated the Irish poet's sense of the magical nature of his craft. This is surely a matter of one dedicated craftsman recognising another.

> God be praised who ne'er forgets me
> In my art so high and cold
> And still sheds upon my verses
> All the magic of red and gold.

He also brought the satirical comedy of the past to life in his translation of Bryan Merryman's long poem, *The Midnight Court*. Reading these translations, one appreciates why 'the backward look' was for O'Connor not just a source of valuable information but an act of instruction in the true meaning of civilisation, a meaning which, unfortunately, gets tragically lost from time to time in Ireland. Scouring the villages, small towns and cities of Ireland, exploring the fields, laneways, byroads and boggy places of the country in the early 1940 O'Connor was engaged in a passionate search for that civilisation. The fact that many people thought he was a bit dotty merely deepened both his determination and his humour, because easy mockery will always add salt to a genuine passion.

In the rather mysterious matter of individual vision, a writer on a bicycle is in a privileged position. If he were in a car, he would of course move more quickly but see infinitely less, because cars, being potentially deadly weapons as well as useful vehicles, demand constant attention from the driver. Cars are, in fact, very greedy for attention and will play nasty tricks if they don't get it. People who for whatever reason become drivers of cars miss out on many of life's passing glories. But a man or a woman on a bicycle has the opportunity to turn aside from travelling to witness and savour these same glories in a deeply pleasurable and unhurried way. *Irish Miles* proves that the best way, after walking, to see a country, to taste its glories, to know its people in all their relaxed foibles, prejudices and charms, is to cycle through that country, making hourly excursions into surprise, learning once again the pleasure of strange personalities, now spontaneous, now suspicious, but almost always fascinating. There is only one puncture in *Irish Miles*; and the fixing of that puncture is in itself a memorable little drama. One of my responses to re-reading this book was a quick mental act of gratitude to whoever invented the bicycle. He helped to quicken and vary individual vision, and therefore literature. He put perception on wheels.

*Irish Miles* is packed with precise (often shatteringly precise) perceptions about Ireland's people and culture, especially its archaeology and popular attitudes or non-attitudes to it. Like Joyce, Yeats and Patrick Kavanagh, O'Connor knows the Irish to the bone. 'Protestant and Catholic, we are as decent a race of people as you are likely to find, but without the black of your nail of any instinct for conserving things.' Imagine a man of O'Connor's passion for the past, cycling hungrily through the rainy landscape, endlessly encountering people sublimely, absurdly or callously indifferent to his passion, and you have a good idea of the comedy of this book. I always have the image of a passionate pilgrim managing at best to amuse sceptical waysiders. Indeed, one of the deepest delights of *Irish Miles* is the series of encounters between O'Connor and various people he meets on the way. These encounters sometimes happen in or near what's left of some old church or castle or tower, or else in a pub or shop or private house. O'Connor's companions on the journey, his wife Evelyn and his friend Stan Stewart, are renamed like gorgeously-dressed creatures from some Molière comedy (one cannot avoid the thought that Molière would have relished a bit of madness in Cork or Connemara), and these exotic-sounding fellow-travellers, Célimène, Géronte, Angélique, Orgon, coming into contact with local characters all over Ireland, add considerably to the deep humour of the book. But it is O'Connor's ear for dialogue, for subtle turns of phrase, for emotional undertones, kind or bitchy implications, cross-currents of allusion as well as his unerring eye for character that helps to account for the many funny moments in *Irish Miles*. Such moments do more than offer relief from the main thrust of varying degrees of beauty and ugliness; they also show O'Connor's compulsion to humanise all this experiences. He believes that 'the shabbiness of Irish life has turned us all into introverts; from Swift's day to Yeats' there have been few Irishmen who knew how to use their eyes.' There is some truth in this, but what is indisputably true is that he uses his eyes in a shrewd, cool, accurate way and brings alive what he sees in a touching and convincing manner. One of my favourite passages in this book occurs when O'Connor, feeling rather sad, gives a lift to his heart by having a conversation with an ivy-covered tower of the Church of Ireland persuasion. This is typical O'Connor comedy – humane, charming, with a serious critical undercurrent.

'What the hell brought us to this hole?' I asked aloud.
'It's all very well for you,' the tower replied unexpectedly.
'You can get out of it in the morning, but I have to stay on here.'
'Congregations bad?' I asked.
'Rotten,' said the tower. 'The Church of Ireland is going to the devil. All the decent people seem to be leaving the country.'
'I know,' said I. 'And as the woman in Myshall told us, "Everybody can be done without, but at the same time they're missed."'
'For God's sake did you see what the other fellows are after building round the corner?' asked the tower, referring, I knew, to the Augustinian church.

'We did glance in,' I said cautiously, for as an agnostic I dislike getting mixed up in sectarian disputes.

'And the grand old abbey church behind that they've let go to rack and ruin,' sighed the tower.

'We didn't see that,' said I. 'The monks have the place sown with wheat.'

'Talking about wheat,' said the tower, 'couldn't you do something about this ivy?'

'I have the hands cut off myself already, pulling down ivy,' I explained apologetically. 'Of course, I could write to the Board of Works for you.'

'Board of Works! Board of Works!' snorted the tower.

'Isn't it they have me the way I am? I don't know what your politics are, young man, but I say this country has no future. No future!'

Because he humanises whatever he possibly can, O'Connor feels that 'love must be a little finer and intenser with a cathedral, a castle or a Tudor courtyard to echo its whispers in the dusk.' Always, with O'Connor, I get the feeling that he is drawn to the ruins of beautiful buildings because they suggest noble feelings, noble dreams. And this search for nobility of feeling and form runs through his fiction also. Even in the murderous atmosphere of war, in a story like *Guests of the Nation*, for example, he tries to locate and define the nature of friendship. As he encounters banality, loneliness, envy, frustration and boredom, he longs for a beautiful context that will nurture and encourage feelings of love and tolerance as well as the capacity to admire and praise. This sensuous, imaginative yearning helps to explain his extraordinary ability to evoke what is for him the essential spirit of any particular place in Ireland, be it Dublin, Cork, Limerick, Kilkenny or some decrepit village in the back of beyond.

It is not an exaggeration to say that in this book O'Connor captures in a quite magical way the complex spirit of Ireland itself. I don't simply mean the spirit of the magnificent old ruins or the spirit of the people with their wandering minds, lazy ways and animated talk, or the spirit of the scattered cities, towns and villages. I mean the spirit of the land itself in all its bewildering changes of mood in sun and rain and light and dark and half-light, of an ambiguous, shifting landscape, peaceful at one moment, then quickly restless, then calm again, then suddenly turbulent and stormy. O'Connor's prose, always agile and pointed, captures that ambiguity and these quick changes in a style that can be at times, like the landscape itself, breathtakingly beautiful. Beautiful, yes; but also almost unbearably desolate and lonely.

It was showery, typically Connemara weather. Sometimes for long spells everything went black out and the mountains disappeared entirely behind a wall of rain. Then came a curious feeling of suspense, and suddenly the hillside on our right began to glow, a single chalky glimmer like the spotlight in a theatre. The chalky spot moved; it flashed upon the road, and, in the bare brown fields at the other side, black-and-red cows were cut out of the landscape with extraordinary vividness. It swept across the margin of a lake and turned it a brilliant blue. The mountains still remained invisible and the sky above them was streaked with a muddy brown stain, but even as one looked at it the veil of rain began to grow transparent, dazzling, spinning threads of it, and behind it we saw, not so much the mountains themselves but the shadow of clouds on the mountains; and then, as the lighting was stepped up and the cloud shadows grew clearer, you saw, in faint blue pencil lines like veins, the planes of the mountain, with silver flashes that crossed them from torrents in flood. It was wonderful, theatrical to the last degree, but lonesome beyond belief.

Fabulous changes, real beauty, real loneliness – these are some elements of that spirit evoked by O'Connor. He is lyrical in his celebration of Ireland's beauty; he is ruthless in his portrayal of Irish bitterness, begrudgery, mindless violence, savage prejudice and craw-thumping hypocrisy. At one point in his travels, he meets two charming people, the tailor and his wife, Anstey. In a paragraph, O'Connor tells us what a censorious Government did to this innocent, imaginative old man.

And there, by the road, with his withered leg stretched out, his round, yellow, baby face, his piercing little eyes, was the Tailor, teaching Irish to a couple of city children. He was a little leprechaun of man, a rural Dr. Johnson. A couple of years ago, a young visitor from England wrote down some of his stories and sayings, and then the old man's troubles really began. The book was banned by the Irish Government as 'indecent', Government spokesmen described him as 'a dirty old man', and a gang of priests made him burn the book at his own hearth.

Only this year, 1987, a book, *The Joy Of Sex*, by the English writer Alex Comfort was banned in Ireland. Some of the more unpleasant aspects of Irish life depicted by O'Connor are sadly still with us.

The overwhelming impression of *Irish Miles*, however, is of a wonderfully fresh, humane, intelligent and warm-hearted book. Written out of a deep love, at once critical and appreciative, it has the effect of opening new doors into Irish life, history, myth, architecture and archaeology. To read it is to embark on a thoroughly delightful journey in the company of a wise, laughing man who keeps one informed and amused from beginning to end. He also moves one deeply from time to time. When *Irish Miles* is read and the journey over, the reader-traveller will feel relaxed and renewed, his mind and soul refreshed with images of an ancient civilisation seen through the eyes of a writer whose humanity flows warmly through this packed, penetrating book.

*Brendan Kennelly, Dublin, 1987*

*Light Dying*

In Memoriam Frank O'Connor (Michael O'Donovan)

Climbing the last steps to your house, I knew
That I would find you in your chair,
Watching the light die along the canal,
Recalling the glad creators, all
Who'd played a part in the miracle.
A silver-haired remembering king, superb there
In dying light, all ghosts being at your beck and call,
You made them speak as only you could do

Of generosity or loneliness or love
Because, you said, all men are voices, heard
In the pure air of the imagination.
I hear you now, your rich voice deep and kind,
Rescuing a poem from time, bringing to mind
Lost centuries with a summoning word,
Lavishing on us who need much more of
What you gave, glimpses of heroic vision.

So you were angry at the pulling down
Of what recalled a finer age; you tried
To show how certain things destroyed, ignored,
Neglected was a crime against the past,
Impoverished the present. Some midland town
Attracted you, you stood in the waste
Places of an old church and, profoundly stirred,
Pondered how you could save what time had sorely
    tried.

Or else you cried in rage against the force
That would reduce to barren silence all
Who would articulate dark Ireland's soul;
You knew the evil of the pious curse,
The hearts that make God pitifully small
Until He seems the God of little fear
And not the God that you desired at all;
And yet you had the heart to do and dare.

I see you standing at your window,
Lifting a glass, watching the dying light
Along the quiet canal bank come and go
Until the time has come to say good-night.
You see me to the door; you lift a hand
Half-shyly, awkwardly, while I remark
Your soul's fine courtesy, my friend, and
Walk outside, alone, suddenly in the dark.

But in the dark or no, I realise
Your life's transcendent dignity,
A thing more wonderful than April skies
Emerging in compelling majesty,
Leaving mad March behind and making bloom
Each flower outstripping every weed and thorn.
Life rises from the crowded clay of doom.
Light dying promises the light re-born.

# I

EXPLORING the Boyne Valley in the early days of our married life, before we yet knew what we were looking for and when anything from a high cross to a keep could lure us off our road, Célimène and I came on the prehistoric necropolis of Newgrange. Prehistory or high crosses, all were the same to us. It was a showery day, and after cycling a mile and a half in the rain to find the caretaker so kindly provided by the Board of Works, we found he had already gone back to the tombs with a couple of military officers. We returned. The rain cleared off as quickly as it had begun, and the blue plains of Meath sparkled and steamed all round us, and there in the heart of them was the great tumulus, overgrown with grass and bushes, and surrounded by its circle of monoliths. The two officers were there, but the caretaker had gone off to find some candles — the Board of Works, as we learned later, hasn't yet heard of electric light and will probably drop dead when it does. Dwarfed by the tall stones with their mysterious patterns, the two young men, one plump and cheery, the other slim and good-looking, looked damned unhistoric. Somehow you could never imagine them turning into spirals and trumpets in the National Museum or being lectured on as a style or period. We nodded to one another and tried not to look too self-conscious, but all the same the atmosphere was rather like that of a doctor's waiting-room. The slim officer broke the silence in a rather startling way.

'I wonder would you consider it — what's the word ? — if I said this was Egyptian ?'

'It's been called a lot of things in its time,' I replied, so taken aback that I broke into a Belfast accent which made the other officer hoot with delight. He obviously thought I was a great card.

'Up the Six Counties !' he said.

'No, but I mean it,' the first officer went on eagerly — he was a different type entirely ; clever and highly-strung. 'I understand that all these spirals and things are really sun symbols.'

'I think you'd be quite safe in calling them anything,' said I. 'You couldn't very well be contradicted.'

'Oh, yes,' he said, by no means satisfied with the reply. 'I read that in a book somewhere. I wish I could remember the name of it. It's the same thing as you find in the Pyramids.'

We were interrupted by the caretaker bringing back the bits of sacred candle which looked as if they might be contemporary, and we solemnly lit them and crawled after him through the depths of the hillside, under the great half-human shoulders of crude stone, giving ourselves a crick in the neck while we tried to study the patterns on them. In the central chamber we were able to stand, and the officer flicked his torch rapidly up the walls to the roof. I knew I ought to feel moved, but while I tried to remember that this was the heart of Irish prehistory, I found myself watching the shadows which the candle-light threw on the young, warm, eager faces. The second officer didn't seem to be altogether sure of himself, and waited for me to make another joke just to reassure him that history didn't apply to him. Personally, at that moment I very much doubted if it did. I felt sure he would get out of it somehow. But his friend was absolutely determined on the point.

'It was the Milesians who built this, wasn't it ? ' he asked, looking about him.

'It's supposed to have been the Tuatha De Danann,' said I. 'Whoever the blazes the Tuatha De Danann were.'

'That's right,' he said quickly. 'They were priestly johnnies, weren't they ? '

'At any rate, the people who came after them adopted them as gods,' said I.

'That's just the same thing that happened in Crete,' he said. 'Crete was a daughter-civilisation of Egypt. It was started by a priestly caste, just like the Tuatha De Danann, and then the Dorians came and booted them out. The Dorians were soldiers.

2

That's how civilisation began. It's all in a book I read once, but I can't remember the name of it. Can you?'

'No,' I said firmly, 'I can't.'

'But that's what happened here all right,' he said with conviction. 'The Milesians were a military caste; they came from the Mediterranean, and booted out the priestly johnnies and took over the show.'

I was just on the point of suggesting that I didn't notice any shortage of priestly johnnies, but decided that, having once talked in a Belfast accent, the less I had to say about the clergy the better. The other officer mightn't understand that I was joking.

'That's how civilisation began,' the first officer continued eagerly, 'with priests and soldiers. It all centres on the Mediterranean. The first time it happened was on the banks of the Nile. A lot of priestly johnnies learned to calculate the time of the Nile floods so that they could have three crops of wheat instead of one. It's all in that book I've been telling you about if only I could remember the name.'

I was just as glad he couldn't. I shouldn't have been able to believe in its existence. History simply vanished before the pair of them with their eagerness and good looks. I had no doubt it must be subjective. We left them with real regret, and cycled on uphill through a wooded glen, and downhill again into a secluded valley. This was Mellifont, Honey Fountain, St. Malachy's first settlement in his attempt to Europeanise the Irish Church. A French master-builder had supervised its erection, but his monks and the Irish monks didn't agree on the principles of architecture, so after some time they returned to France. But he must, I believe, have been still in Ireland at the time of the consecration, and seen all the famous figures of the tragedy which led up to the Norman invasion. They were all there : O'Connor, the last Irish king; his ruffianly lieutenant, O'Rourke, with his middle-aged wife Darvorgilla, and her lover-to-be, Diarmuid MacMurrough, prince of Leinster, a ruffian even more abominable than her husband. A pretty gang of thieves they were, and Brother Robert of Citeaux must have had a rare time showing

3

them the marvels of this new type of architecture. Up to this, they had seen nothing but the little churches of out-of-the-way monasteries which they were so fond of burning, but this great type of Cistercian architecture with its massive walls and vaulted roofs must have posed them some nice problems in arson. Not that we saw much of it. There was a ruined tower on the right, a tiny, ruined parish church on the side of the hill, an old mill where they sold picture postcards, and the octagon of a lavabo in beautiful European Romanesque. They were cutting the hay, and perhaps if we had come a day later we might have seen a bit more of the lay-out, but now there was nothing to assist us except a big blue notice-board, the contents of which I had to read to Célimène, who fondly believed that there ought to be something to guide us. It ran :

' " Abstract of a Letter of the Lord Abbot of Mount St. Joseph, Roscrea, dated June 10th, 1929, to Very Rev. Francis Canon ——, P. P. Mellifont.

' " Mellifont Abbey Items.

' " 3,000,000 Masses celebrated, Community assembled in Choir 1,160,000 times to say Divine Praises, 4 Bishops, 2 of them Archbishops of Armagh, 25 Abbots and 3,000 Monks buried in Monastery. These Items—— " '

' " Items " is good," interrupted Célimène.

' " These Items ",' I continued firmly, ' " have been Drawn Up by a Young Monk who was asked to make a *Special* Study of your Questions." '

' Is he in the Board of Works too ? ' asked Célimène.

' His father was a labouring man in regular employment,' I added.

' Is that there ? ' she asked in surprise, screwing up her eyes to look at the board.

' No,' I said. ' I just made it up.'

That sprightly pair of lads had cast a spell on the day. We went on to Monasterboice, skipping back a couple of centuries to the days of the Culdees. They were making the hay there too. We looked for a while at the beautiful old crosses, and then had our lunch and fell fast asleep propped up against a grave. We might of course have dreamed of some old abbot or stone-cutter, in which case this chapter would have been much more exciting, but the fact is that we didn't dream at all. There was no history on us, and in the cool of the evening we cycled under awnings of blue shadow into the little village of Slane. It was dark on the steep road down to the river, with its great avenue of trees and Gothic gateway. By the bridge was a handsome old mill and mill-house, and the great span of the slow, sedgy Boyne. On the far bank a few country boys were playing pitch-and-toss by the light of an electric torch.

We went back and stood in the Square. In the whole Square there are only four houses; four three-storey houses set back a little from the four corners, with flanking walls leading to pavilions in the shape of coach-houses, each facing on to a different road. There were two wrought-iron lanterns in each roadway. That was all; four houses, eight coach-houses, sixteen arches, eight lanterns; and even then the lanterns are now only stumps, the arches hidden with shrubbery. One house belongs to the police, another to the doctor, while the parish priest's house has had its roof raised, and its little Georgian panes replaced by stained glass.

But it is clear that the architect had another story in mind when he found the solution to the problem of his Square. I feel sure it was a love story, and that from one of the small-paned Georgian windows he intended some woman to look out night after night on the eight lanterns which shut in her little world, and the carriages that rolled in and out of it with their officers, duellists and squireens from Trim and Drogheda. Was she married, and, if so, for whom did he intend the other two houses? Was it perhaps one of the four-sided comic intrigues that eighteenth-century dramatists delighted in? The sense of the past swooped down and enveloped us. Below on the river-bank it all began, ages and ages ago, with priestly johnnies and soldier johnnies, and all the trouble they started hasn't yet come to an end.

I feel sure the architect's tale had a happy ending, for though the Gothic gateway under the trees may have been in existence, it had not yet set the fashion for unhappy love, Shelley's poetry and Robert Emmet's speech from the dock. Wolfe Tone, rationalism and married love were still the rage, and I fancy the architect saw a carriage waiting one night on the road down to the river, a coach-house door opening quietly, and a young woman tripping out with lifted skirts. Then a few whispered words, and the carriage rattled over the bridge in the direction of Dublin.

So, at least I fancy, but it is all hard to read, and it is only when darkness falls, and the four old houses cease to whisper correct, serious, official things to one another about the decline in morals and the decay of children's teeth, compulsory Irish and the licensing of dogs, that the old wrought-iron lanterns seem to glow again, the four houses become a string quartet, and the tune they play a Boccherini minuet or a Mozart serenade, melancholy and gay.

YELLOW, broken-backed, heavy with history, the dese-
crated market cross of Kells filled the opening of the clean,
pale, decorous Georgian street like a lifted finger. Tradition says
it was used by the English as a gallows, but its ninth- or tenth-
century sculpture is still remote enough. About its base a
procession of horsemen hunted a procession of stags, and above
were Christ crowned and crucified. Within the graveyard with
its fatty green, the yellow, thickly-set crosses seemed like trees,
as though they had been there so long that they had taken root and
drawn their yellow colour from the earth. One had snapped
under the stone-cutter's chisel, for he had left it so, with the
panels merely sketched out, and in one of them the five or six
strokes which were the basis of his simple composition. Behind
it, under the Round Tower, was another cross with another
mysterious procession of huntsmen and stags, and near it a beautifully carved shaft broken off a few feet from the ground.

As we cycled north from the rich Boyne country the land
began to rise ; the grass lost its enamel, and the bare earth its
burnish. In Cavan they still build lovers' seats by the roadside,
and a very pleasant custom it seemed when the three of us,
Géronte, Célimène and I, sat down to lunch. We were only a
mile or so inside the Cavan boundary, and already there was a
blue lake at the foot of the field, and the little hills, continuous
and rolling like a grey, wintry sea, began to tumble on top of
one another, with the dark curves of the fences echoing the folds
in the land ; while here and there some roller, pinched at the top
into a narrow spine like the crown of a soft hat, broke into a thin
dark foam of rock.

It was beautiful country, crabbed and stunted and grey, like
an orchard full of old apple trees ; country for a draughtsman,
not for a painter, for nothing interrupted that continuous subtle

variation of pattern except where some fool from a Government office had planted a belt of pines : nothing cloyed as in Kerry or Connemara ; the country moved with us ; the roads, climbing and dropping and insinuating themselves between the scooped-out troughs of the grey rollers, produced a constant sense of gentle animation ; and it was only at the top of a hill where two screens of rock-crested hillside drew back from the road that we could sit down to tea, and watch through the gap the immense distance of bumpy Tuscan hills among which the sunlight fell in long shafts, pale as the ghosts of primroses.

Yet it must be the devil's own country to live in, and perhaps it seems so much poorer than Connemara because it has none of Connemara's theatrical magic, and so has more power of getting on top of the inhabitants, but I swear I have never seen such filthy houses. Even in the wildest spots of Connemara you will find fuchsia hedges, flowers, colour-wash and crimson paint ; but in Cavan the only traditional colour seems to be a dirty Reckitt's blue, and even that they only buy by the half-ounce.

Fine two-storey houses, twice the size of a Connemara cabin, had never been whitewashed or painted since the day they were built ; there were dung-heaps in front of the doors, and scraps of lace curtains in the windows which were almost as black as the windows themselves. Yet the country was thinly populated, the land well tilled ; there was breeding in the tall hexagonal gate-posts ; and in the hollows among the bog-pools the turf clamps were neatly thatched with fresh straw and weighted with rows of sods. In one tilled field, not much bigger than a respectable blanket, there was a cottage about the size of a night-ark for chickens, complete even to the chimney-pot, and apparently all made out of bits of tin can. No, it wasn't all poverty or even thriftlessness. I got the impression of thrift and cunning gone a bit soft in the head and hugging itself in barren ecstasies of economy.

The crows woke us next morning, and, when I raised the blinds, there was a regiment of them storming about the ruined tower of the Protestant church. Cavan town falls drunkenly about in a mid-Atlantic of little hills, and over the chimney-pots, going up hill and down dale, were sunlit green rollers, all rearing themselves on their hind legs to catch a glimpse of us. We had to cycle out to the Protestant cathedral which some bishop of the last century rebuilt on the slope of a hill convenient to Lord Farnham's front gate. As a cathedral there is nothing much wrong with it. It is very large and very handsome in a nineteenth-century restorer's style, and it is perhaps only a detail that it is three miles from the nearest town. Possibly the bishop argued that, as it was only a Protestant cathedral, it didn't matter ; possibly he felt that no true Protestant could possibly be without his carriage and pair. It may have been the same man who brought the fine Romanesque doorway from an island church a couple of miles out in the lake and rebuilt it in the north wall of the cathedral, for he did it with such enthusiasm that he had no time to put the stones together as he found them. Originally, I suspect, it must have had pilasters instead of shafts. While I was photographing it a melancholy-looking gardener came and watched me. He assured me that the last person whom he had allowed to photograph that doorway — a lady with a three-legged arrangement for her camera — had given him a half-sovereign.

We were sitting in the hotel having coffee when the door opened and two men shuffled in. At first I took them to be a farmer and a drover, but then I realised that they were really father and son. It was market day in town and they were the only country people who came in, so I marked them down as individualists. The old man came in without raising his eyes or his knees, as if he were pushing some weight before him with his belly, like an engine. They sat down at a glass-topped table, the old man taking off his hat and laying it on a chair beside him. He had a glib of white hair which reached to the bridge of his nose, and a Punchinello chin. His son had the same sort of glib, but it was brown. He too took off his cap and put it on the remaining chair, but he was less a man of the world than his father, and as if he thought it might be considered

9

presumptuous, or perhaps unsafe, or even that he might be charged extra for occupying the chair, he took it back and stowed it away on the ground beneath him.

I watched the pair of them in fascination. There they sat, slumped in their chairs with their arms hanging by their sides, staring intently at the glass top of the table, like two mountains overlooking a lake. One or other of them must have ordered something, though it seemed to me that they didn't, and that the order was understood. The waitress first brought a loaf and the younger man steadily cut slice after slice until it was all cut up. She brought a bowl of soup for the older man who slowly broke several slices of bread into it. She brought a cup of tea for the other, and he buttered one slice of bread, only to find himself with a bit of butter left on his knife which he didn't know what to do with. He looked at it steadily for a while, and then, having a brain-wave, he buttered himself a second slice. After that he took good care not to experiment any further with the butter but saucered his tea. They never spoke during the whole meal, but when they had finished, and there wasn't crust or crumb of the loaf remaining, the old man took a dirty cloth purse from his trousers pocket and handed the young man a coin. The young man looked at it in astonishment. 'Is it a bob a head?' he muttered. 'Don't know what it is,' replied the other.

Those now, so far as I could gather, were the only words uttered by either of them, so I feel that they are important enough to be placed on record. The young man retrieved his cap, put it on and went into the kitchen. He returned a few minutes later with what appeared to be a sixpenny bit and a few coppers and stood by his own chair turning them over and over as he looked at them. Maybe he was trying to do the sum, or maybe he was wondering whether he oughtn't to ask his father for the change. I do not know what wild schemes may have been passing through his mind at that moment. He may even have been thinking of buying a packet of cigarettes — he was only about thirty-five and capable of any flightiness. His father ignored him, and went on looking at the table, still masticating in the manner of the late Mr. Gladstone. He wasn't in the least uneasy. Probably he had had other sons. He knew all young men were wild like that at least once in their lives. They all settled down in time.

At last the young man gave it up ; cast a longing look at the money and returned it. Without looking up the old man took it, put his hand in his trousers pocket, took out the big cloth purse and quietly put back the change. They went out exactly as they had come in, the old man still masticating, and I followed them with my eyes till they disappeared up the street. I felt exactly as if someone had punctured me and left me slowly dissolving through the legs of my trousers.

I never rightly recovered from the shock for the rest of the day. It was market day and the town was full. In the town park, as it must once have been called, a very Roman-looking Lord Farnham who was supposed to have been killed in a railway accident was disappearing for the last time under a sea of weeds. A little further up the street they were putting the finishing touches to a new Catholic cathedral in the classical style of Mullingar, with tiled pavements and flights of steps, groups of very smooth statuary in the pediment, and a tower vaguely reminiscent of something on the Strand.

Two out-of-works who were admiring it told us it had cost a quarter of a million to build. I couldn't get the father and son out of my head. The church seemed to me a sort of sublimation of them, and when I looked up at the tower—really, when you came to consider it, so very unlike anything on the Strand—it seemed to be decorated with thousands of little gold streamers that fluttered out north, south, east and west, into every little stony glen and every seedy farmhouse that hadn't seen a lick of paint since the day it was built ; and each streamer earthed itself in the cloth purse in the trousers pocket of an old farmer who stood, looking out from his doorway at the dunghill, chewing with Punchinello jaws while he thought long and melancholy thoughts about the scarcity of feeding stuffs, the flightiness of the younger generation, and the price of wheat.

## 3

DUBLIN was once one of the art capitals of Europe. Perhaps from an aeroplane flying low it might still seem to be one with its broad rosy streets of Georgian and its spires and domes. But when one descended and returned through the streets themselves one would see the women sitting on the doorsteps and the mobs of barefooted, half-savage children playing in the gutted hallways. Take Henrietta Street for instance, once one of the most fashionable streets in Europe. It was built by a German called Cassells ; heavy in the hand, uncertain in his proportions, and capable of giving everything he did a certain funereal air.

I don't want to crab the man, because he built Russborough, to me the most beautiful of Irish country houses. It lies twenty-odd miles outside Dublin on the main road beyond the Poulaphouca Hydro-Electrical Works, facing the great new artificial lake and the mountains where it gathers, an eighteenth-century house out of fairyland. The only other house I know which has the same startling effect is Castletown, near Celbridge, and the only way I can explain it to myself is that it was some accidental quality of architecture before Classicism became complete. After that the difference between a masterpiece and a commonplace is only a neck ; the odds is gone, and I have enough of the gambling instinct in me to rejoice when some horse, preferably not the favourite, leaves the rest of the field trotting. It was the outsider Cassells who took this house, modest enough in proportion, and scattered it recklessly across the landscape, with its colonnades, its long pavilions and its fairy-tale stable gates, until its civilisation is a match for the mountain wildness.

But Henrietta Street is a different kettle of fish ; a little hill leading to the cul-de-sac of Gandon's King's Inns ; tall houses tall flights of steps, leading to tall narrow doorways too small for the frontage and with a heavy hooded air imparted by their plain pediments. The only houses which have not degenerated into slum are the two on the right-hand side by the gate of King's Inns, and these have been turned into convents. The front has been cemented, and Cassells' gloomy doorway has been removed to make way for a gay Egyptian one in imitation marble. One slum house attracted us because a first-floor window had been lifted out, body and bones, and through it you could see the staircase ceiling, heavy circles and strapwork which suggested a Jacobean hang-over. The poor people sunning themselves on the steps drew aside to let us pass. The staircase had been many times coated with salmon-coloured wash which half obscured the rich plaster panelling, but a ray of light through a ruined window-frame lit a beautiful stair with carved treads and delicate Restoration newel-posts. It would have been all right but for the smell.

'The convent, at any rate, will be clean,' said I.

The door was opened for us by an exquisite, smiling creature in a flapping veil who was delighted to show us everything. The parlour, with a ceiling in the same overpowering design of circles and straps, pedimented wall panels, a marble fireplace, a great pedimented door leading into the front room, was the sort of place you dream of. There were two exquisite doors leading out of it into the hall with little cupids set above them in a sort of undesigned composition which delighted me. The fine stairs were placed at the back of the house, which meant that the saloon — now a chapel — was in the front. It looked as if it had received Egyptian attention. The fine ceiling was painted blue and gold, and in a bright blue window over the altar was a scraggy-looking Madonna. The adorable little nun was on her knees. I could see that Célimène, who is emotional, was already half-way to becoming a Catholic, and foresaw trouble in the home.

'You should try to see our house next door,' said the nun as we were leaving. 'The nuns' dining-room has a lovely ceiling.'

She said it in a doubtful tone as though she were afraid we shouldn't find our way. We soon saw why. Here the hall with wooden pillars painted to imitate marble, was in front. The ceiling of the staircase with beautiful girls' heads at the four sides, was superb. A middle-aged woman was sitting at a table as if collecting the admission fee.

'I'll have to see the sister in charge,' she said.

By this time Célimène's conversion was almost complete. As the minutes passed and lengthened into a quarter of an hour, I could see the old Calvinistic Methodist streak beginning to emerge, and realised that the danger of domestic friction was lessening. The image of the nun next door was beginning to fade. Fully twenty minutes passed before we heard a slow step on the stairs and, looking up, we saw against the great panelled ceiling the fluttering of a veil. The nun made a magisterial half-circle about us as though afraid of coming into contact with our worldly aura and then faced us from the other side of the table. She didn't like us ; neither did she like our errand.

'This is all we have to show,' she said severely. 'And you've seen that,' she added. She looked about her without interest. 'Eighteenth century, I believe ?'

'Just so,' said I.

'Or is it seventeenth ?'

'Eighteenth,' said I, and we took our leave before Célimène could say what she thought. Célimène interprets altogether too literally the text about 'knowing them by their fruits'. The conversion hadn't taken, and she was again a black, raging Calvinistic Methodist, contemptuous of all idolaters. We dived into the first house which attracted us. Smells no longer seemed the principal evil. We knocked, and a pleasant, worried little woman answered. The front room on the ground floor had been partitioned off at shoulder height into a tiny hallway which housed a pram, a bedroom and a living-room. The bedroom had overflowed into the living-room in a double bed, and the rest of the space was taken up with pathetic little knick-knacks, including just inside the 'doorway' a cupboard with a big glass case, containing a statue of the Blessed Virgin. Above hallway, living-room and bedroom stretched a whitewashed ceiling, and in the centre, smiling down upon everything, was a splendid head of Apollo with a spike driven clean through the forehead as though at some time the Gas Company had connected and then disconnected him. 'The Crucifixion,' Géronte said, when I brought him to see it later.

Strange fates have overtaken the gods and goddesses of Dublin. The Jesuits of Belvedere House have retained their Apollo but Venus has been cut away. The priests in St. Saviour's Orphanage, once the home of the plasterer Robert West, in Dominick Street, have been more tolerant, and even in their chapel the ceiling shows two naked cupids, as Love and Eternity, or some such heathen allegory, while next door the little waifs look up from the plain iron beds of their dormitory and see Venus wantoning naked with Cupid and doves. Mespil House was deserted when we visited it. The front door was open, and the rooms were empty. In the back room, darkened by creeper which had forced its way through the shutters, was the most beautiful of Irish ceilings. Jupiter held the centre in a rolling mass of cloud, which bellows-cheeked cherubs puffed up at him from the four quarters, where the elements were shown in exquisite panels : Earth with her castled crown and lion, Water with her urn, Wind with her clouds and Fire with her salamander.

But even in the most respectable streets where the shadow of poverty has never fallen, you cannot guess which of the immortals is housed with what unlikely companions. Ely Place, for instance, is an unexceptionable neighbourhood. For preference Célimène and I chose the largest and richest-looking house. We wondered what it was ; it looked as though it probably was a Government Department. But when we turned the handle and got into the front hall we found ourselves faced by an inner door, a bell and a warning notice that under no circumstances were non-members admitted beyond this door.

Clearly this was a club, and a very exclusive sort of club at that. I fingered a half-crown in my pocket as I rang the bell. A respectable man with a kind and melancholy expression answered the door ; obviously not the sort of person you could bribe. A different approach was called for.

'I'm afraid,' he said with regret, ' we are exceedingly strict about allowing visitors. What is the name, please ? '

I told him. I admit that for once I allowed vanity to get the better of me, but when it comes to wheedling my way into houses which may contain works of art, I have now become capable of any baseness : bribery, boasting or out-and-out false-hood. Nothing corrupts the character like a passion for archi-tecture. And sometimes a little vanity goes a long way. When we went to see Tyrone House, the headquarters of the Ministry of Education, we were shown round by minister and officials as if we were royalty. When a policeman came to arrest us in Freshford for taking photographs in war-time, I had no sooner mentioned my name than he wrung me warmly by the hand and assured me that the Sergeant would be heart-broken at missing me. But I was well punished for my vanity, because it was quite clear that the Secretary, or whoever it was, had never heard of me.

'If you'll step inside a moment,' he said courteously, ' I'll see what can be done.'

We stepped inside, and made the acquaintance of Hercules. Hercules, life size, was acting as newel-post of the great staircase which, instead of banisters, had long gilded beasts who slunk up the stairs to the first-floor landing. Against the Venetian window which lit the well of the stairs was a shadowy figure supporting a cross, and on the wall on our left a big picture of the Pope looking at Hercules. Along the wall of the stairs was a row of pencil drawings by Sean O'Sullivan of distinguished-looking men whom I failed to recognise.

The Secretary returned and to our relief agreed to let us see the house. He was an intelligent and sensitive man, and though he affected to know nothing of architecture, was obviously proud of it. He said it was the town house of the Earl of Ely and had previously belonged to Sir Thornley Stoker, the surgeon. Then I remembered that it figures quite a lot in George Moore's *Hail and Farewell*, for Moore and Gogarty were both near neighbours and friends of Sir Thornley.

Apart from the stairs it wasn't really a first-rate job. The front room on the ground floor, painted an olive green, had large plaster medallions linked by Adamsish scroll-work, and seemed like the work of Michael Stapleton, the Irish contemporary of Adams. There was a fireplace with another Hercules which the Secretary told us was insured for £700. The sun suddenly went out in the claret-coloured street, and a lovely subdued light brought up the modelling of the plaster figures in the medallions. I rested my camera on a side table, and noticed, without much interest, that the tablecloth was black. I do not mean dirty, but black.

There were three rooms on the first floor, all decorated. The one in the centre was a small waiting-room with two very pleasant medallions in low relief. There was a plain screen across it half-way down, and behind this a table in front of the window. The room on the right was large, and had a number of small tables like that in the downstairs room, and these, too, had black tablecloths. What appeared to be a door was lying across a couple of chairs, and when we entered the Secretary, as I must continue to call him, lifted it and put it back against the wall, where it fitted over the original mahogany door. There was a crucifix on the fine white-and-yellow mantelpiece.

I stood before one of the medallions in the little waiting-room wondering whether I shouldn't photograph it. The Secretary noticed my eyes fixed on it.

'Of course, that's only a copy,' he said. 'It's really only canvas.'

'Oh, indeed?' said I, and looking at it more closely I could see that it was merely fitted into the wall and could be taken out without difficulty.

17

'Yes,' he said, 'we often have dances here, and the band sits in this room.'

'How very convenient!' said I, and at that point I began to wonder what there was about a dance band that made it convenient that it should be heard but not seen.

'Is this,' I asked, 'a private club or could people like ourselves become members?'

'Well, it's not exactly a club,' said the Secretary hesitatingly. 'This is the headquarters of the Knights of Columbanus.'

There is a moment in every real thriller when the hero, tracking the missing heroine, finds himself in a quiet house on a quiet street, and on asking the name of his charming and cultured host is told in a gentle voice, 'The name, Mr. Blake, is Plummer,' or words to that effect. This was it. The Knights of Columbanus are the most sinister of Irish secret societies; an enormously wealthy organisation of Catholic professional and business men. Their ritual is modelled on that of the Freemasons; the postulants are initiated in a ceremony in which they are marched blindfold with their hands resting on the shoulders of the man in front, up and down corridors to far-away organ music, and when the masks are removed they find themselves in the presence of hooded men sitting at black-covered tables with a skull before them. I now understood something I had noticed as we entered the little room. On the table behind the screen were some black robes embroidered in gold. I understood all the rest as well: the tablecloths, the crucifixes, the false panel. Exclusive was right.

'We are supposed to be a secret society,' the Secretary went on in a troubled tone. 'After all, we are no more a secret society than any other private company. They don't publish their business. Why should we?'

'Why indeed?' said I.

'Of course,' he said, 'we don't take any oaths or anything like that,' and led the way into the big room to the left of the landing. There was another magnificent but rather ugly fireplace with a lot of tiny medallions in Wedgewood blue and white, looped together in rather inadequate plaster decorations on the walls. Célimène disliked the room and said so, but it was her stern eye which located the harmonium by the door. Her lips framed the word 'band' and her air fully expressed her feelings about the damned idolaters who performed there (You would never think, hearing Célimène on the subject, that her father was a Freemason.)

I started as a bell pealed through the house. Our guide fell silent and waited. We almost counted the heavy steps on the stairs and then a young man appeared and asked for 'Mr. Nolan.' 'He's not in at the moment,' said the Secretary. I do not know what occult meaning was conveyed by those simple words, but I felt enormously relieved when the young man went away. Then I began to be sorry for taking advantage of the Secretary's kindness, ashamed of coming there, as it were like a spy, even though I had declared my identity in the most unequivocal, not to say boastful, manner. He positively wrung my heart when in his courteous way he invited us to come back and look over the house more carefully.

As we went down the stairs I studied the row of pencil drawings on the walls in the hope of identifying a few of the models, while he glanced thoughtfully at the row of gilded beasts whom Hercules was driving up the stairs at the other side.

'I suppose,' he asked, 'you don't know what these beasts are?'

'No,' I replied, looking at the row of portraits, 'I'm afraid I don't recognise any of them.'

Célimène suggested tentatively that one of them was probably a wildebeeste, but I am afraid that was only showing off.

# ❋ 4 ❋

THERE is only one safe rule for travelling in the southern half of Ireland, and that is not to cut across the grain of the country from east to west. South of the midlands, it lies north to south along the great river valleys. It was the rivers and canals which brought Ireland the only period of commercial prosperity it has known, and it is along these that you must look for the big houses and pretty villages.

On the outskirts of Kildare there are two semi-detached red-brick houses, one called 'Simla' and the other 'Lucknow', which show you to what it owed its one-time prosperity, and explain exactly why it vies with the family vault in its attraction for visitors. The pleasantest place in it is the cathedral with its eighteenth-century gate and great chestnut trees. It is half fortress, half church, heavily battlemented, with flights of stone steps over each gable, and arched buttresses which turn the whole exterior into a series of enormous niches. To encourage the faithful, a skull and crossbones from a fifteenth-century tomb has been inserted over the transept door. We heard the organ playing and tiptoed in. Inside the door was a broken Fitzgerald tomb with the effigy, Irish fashion, subsiding through the top. There were only two worshippers in the transept, and I doubt if there were many more in the nave for the doors were locked. The church was wrecked by Cromwell and remains bare and high and unplastered. It made the service sound grim and lonesome, and the Commandments resounded through the bare chancel as though they had originally been uttered from Mount Sinai in a Belfast accent. We didn't like the menacing sound of them and tiptoed out again. The rain had begun to fall softly. We sheltered under a pair of over-arching buttresses, and looked down through the trees at the melancholy road that wandered past a hotel where we had once spent a comfortless night. The only other thing in Kildare is the Japanese Gardens! Wavertree, the race-horse owner, brought over a family of gardeners from Japan to drain the bog and make the finest garden that exists outside of Tokio. One glance at Kildare in the rain makes you appreciate the appropriateness of that.

By the time we had crossed the bog to the canal at Monaster-evan it was pouring cats and dogs. We stood mournfully under the overhanging fascia-board of a pub, and above the other pub on the opposite side of the street a woman's discreet hand drew the curtains an inch or two aside. The people in the huxter shop were less genteel for the woman there leaned her elbows on the sill and stared at us, then stared back up the canal and stared at us again. We were too wet and miserable to care. At last we decided that rain was better than Monasterevan and cycled up by the canal past a row of handsome shuttered houses now falling into decay, and over a hoopsa horseshoe of a bridge where the canal wound back with a glimpse of a lock-keeper's little house. In all the bogland roads from this to the Shannon the best bits are the beautiful old canal bridges and the lock-keepers' cottages. I shall never forget one bridge on the outskirts of Monasterevan with its lock-keeper's cottage, and a barge coming slowly up the canal while a terrier on its bow quivered with impatience as he waited to reach the bridge. As the barge slid beneath us he gave three or four resounding barks, and then waited for the next bridge, and it was quite clear that that terrier's whole idea of happiness con-sisted in travelling on barges and enjoying the echo of his own barking when they passed beneath the bridges.

It wasn't only the wind and rain we got in from when we reached the hotel at Portarlington, which is an old schoolhouse with a grand spaciousness and dignity and a window on the stairs that overlooks the long gardens leading to the river. Even through the rain it was a pleasure to sit in the window of the dining-room and look at the builder's yellow house at the other side of the road, with its sculped-in doorway and unsashed area windows flush with the ground. When the waitress appeared

Célimène said ' Good God ! ' and fell silent. I began to construct the opening phrases of a rigmarole beginning ' *Est-ce que vous pouvez nous donner* ' until I got stuck for the bacon and eggs. Portarlington doesn't leave you for long in doubt as to what part of the world its founders came from.

For all that, it doesn't, as all the guide-books and histories tell you, consist of houses in the French manner, built by Huguenot officers after the Battle of the Boyne. It couldn't possibly have been built within a century of the Battle of the Boyne, and the only thing about it which is particularly French is the uncivil manner in which a few houses above the French church treat the main street as a glorified garden wall, and turn their faces towards the gardens and the river. For the rest it seems to be typically Irish architecture of the canal period. Certainly it is one of the most charming towns in Ireland (though an infernal cinema has now ruined the square). Instead of the usual Georgian street with its severe masses and regular proportions, you get scores and scores of houses in which the proportions have become fluid before dissolving altogether, and where you seem to catch classicism on tiptoe ready for flight ; big houses and little houses ; houses with bow fronts and broad windows, with sculped-in doorways or ornamental frames ; high houses and low houses ; houses that face the road or are turned sideways from the road or turn blank backs altogether on the road.

The rain cleared, and in the summer dusk the doctor was walking about his charming little garden. We introduced ourselves and he gave his name as Dooley. He invited us hospitably to have a look at his house.

' One of the Huguenot houses,' he said. ' They were all built by French officers after the Battle of the Boyne.'

' So they say,' I replied cautiously.

' Oh, it's true. As a matter of fact, I'm half French myself. My mother was a Beauchamp.'

' Indeed,' said I. ' Then you have it both ways.'

' There was a Frenchman here some time ago,' he said, ' writing the history of the colony. He published a book about it afterwards. According to him, my mother's family was actually entitled to the *de*.' The doctor laughed as if it were a very good joke, but I wouldn't have liked to joke with him about it.

'It's quite an honour,' I said.

'Ah, I don't know,' said the doctor jovially, clapping his trousers pocket. 'That's the only thing that counts nowadays, isn't it ?'

I agreed in the same light-hearted way, reflecting privately that neither of us believed it. You can always trust an Irishman who affects to be a materialist. It's the other kind you must watch. As I went out I took the opportunity of glancing at his plate. It said 'Dr. Beauchamp Dooley'.

Portarlington is the prettiest town in this part of Ireland, but it isn't the only one. As it goes on, the Barrow digs itself a deeper and deeper hollow which at Carlow forms a high, pale rampart of hills, tilled and fenced to the top ; a fine background for a typical prosperous river town with handsome little terraces of red brick, painted in the pale blues and greens of the period (a feature which seems to have disappeared everywhere else) ; fine houses along the river-bank, and the tower of a church which distinctly resembles Bruges belfry in galloping consumption. Carlow undoubtedly has an air. Exploring it, we came to a row of whitewashed cottages such as you find on the outskirts of every Irish town, but one of them had been raised a storey and then battlemented on the top. Decidedly it has an air. Ever since Swift labelled it, it has been to the rest of Ireland 'Carlow poor but proud'. We went into a shop in the main street for the makings of our lunch, and the old gentleman behind the counter grew prouder and prouder as Célimène went through her list. It sounded terrible.

'A quarter of butter.' ('Oh, my !')

'A half pound of tomatoes.' ('Well, well !')

'A threepenny box of spreadable cheese.' ('Really, this is too much.')

The old gentleman spread his fingers on the counter, looked

out the shop window with an indescribable air of injured refinement, and murmured inarticulately that his customers usually took larger quantities.

At Killeshin, on the rampart of hills above the town, in what must be one of the dirtiest graveyards in the whole world, were the remains of a twelfth-century church ; two stout, high-peaked gables sprawling down the hill, with the sunlight leaking through a tiny Anglo-Saxon window high above the doorway. The baptismal name of the King of Leinster who founded it, and is commemorated in the inscription above the capitals, mysteriously turns out to be that of no king known to history, which of course gives the antiquarians the chance of their lives.

The doorway itself was in that curious, ungainly, rather Eastern style you find ranged all through the midlands from Kilteely near Dublin to Annaghdown in Co. Galway : squat and bulky with broad pilasters, moulded at the corners, instead of columns, human heads going off into interlacing for capitals, sometimes bulbous bases (even bases with heads on them) and ornament in very low relief. Here every inch of the doorway had been decorated by some leather-worker turned stone-cutter, but itchy goats had wiped it off the pilasters as you might wipe drawings off a blackboard, and the doorway with its lumpish pediment and its variegation of yellow stone seemed a dull and heavy frame for the view of the Barrow valley and the Wicklow hills, whose pale blues and greens twinkled below us in a mist of heat.

We went to look for some place to boil our billy-can. Below the churchyard a man in shirt-sleeves was pacing up and down in the coolness of the hedge before his cottage, his red face shining like a lantern from its shadow.

' 'Tis hot,' he said amicably, brushing away a fly.

' 'Tis then,' said I, ' hot. Could we trouble you to boil our can ? '

' Ye could to be sure,' he said at once. ' Come in, let ye.'

He blew on the fire, but his whole face took on a look of alarm when he saw Célimène putting on the can.

'What are you doing with that, woman?' he cried. 'Take off that lid or you'll smoke the water.'

'Oh, dear,' said Célimène regretfully, 'I never knew that.'

'Now, that's a funny thing,' he said as he took the can from her and balanced it on the fire of sticks. 'When you leave off the lid you'll never get a taste from the water. When myself and the boys are out together at the hay we use that old iron pot there, and not a bit of smoke ever gets near it, no matter what the wind is doing.'

He walked to the door again, tormented by the heat. In front of the fire was a fine home-made armchair with a carved back, and above it a clothes-line made of cotton spools, strung on twine; a dodge I had never seen before. There were three white collars on it, the day being Saturday.

'I'm after doing the week's washing,' he said by way of joke, mistaking the thing that interested me. ''Tis for myself and the two boys. They're out at the hay.'

'Is that all of you there are?' I asked.

'Herself died on me last year,' he said, turning away.

'God help us,' I said, for I knew the way country people grow into one another. ''Tis a great loss.'

''Tis then,' he said with a sigh, 'a great loss. Was it from Carlow direction ye came?'

'It was.'

'Carlow poor but proud,' he said with a mournful shake of his head.

'Why?' I asked in surprise. 'Isn't this County Carlow?'

'It is not,' he replied with an emotion that verged on joy. 'We're just over the Leix border. Oh, that is a mean, miserable, beggarly town,' he went on. 'And since they got the sugar factory there's no standing them. A poor man like me would have no business shopping there at all.'

'And where do you go, then?' I asked.

'Bagenalstown,' he replied.

'Bagenalstown? But that must be ten miles away!'

'Well, the way it is,' he went on, 'it pays me. There is not

25

in that misfortunate town hardly as much as one old decent, established, respectable shopkeeper. 'Tis dosed with strangers : counter-jumpers that came into town and married the master's daughter, and now they'd knock you down with cars the size of the road. . . . Feel that suit I'm wearing,' he added, giving me a handful of the leg of his trousers to grip. 'How much do you think I paid for that suit in Bagenalstown ?'

'I couldn't say.'

'Sixteen shillings,' he said, with a glance at Célimène. 'Two shillings a yard for the stuff and the rest for the making. I have it ten years. If I bought that suit in Carlow 'twould cost me two pounds.'

'Or more,' said I.

'Or more,' he repeated indignantly. 'If you were to put up an old hut by the road and sell tin whistles in Carlow you'd make a fortune. That's if you were a rogue. If you were an honest man you would make nothing. And what in God's name have they to be proud of ? That's what I do be always thinking of. I'd say they were crusted with ignorance. Were you ever in Castlecomer ?'

'Never,' said I.

'Well, now,' he said enthusiastically, 'that's the place you'll go to. 'Tis only nine miles along this road. A grand town ! I was there on the traction. 'Tis there you'd see the miners walking the streets with their faces black from the coal, and the fine, lovely, handsome girls that'd stand that height off the floor for you, walking along beside them with an old shawl over their heads. 'Twould do your heart good. . . . Well, there's the can boiled, and mind what I told you about leaving off the lid !'

'Never fear,' said I. 'We will.'

We ate our meal in the one comparatively clean patch on top of the graveyard wall as we watched the country boys pushing their bicycles up the long hill. Célimène sliced the tomatoes and buttered the bread while I waited for the tea to draw. I was crazy with thirst. Then she poured it out and we both took long swigs. I looked at her and she looked back guiltily at me. I knew she hoped I wouldn't say it, because she had fallen badly for the man in the cottage, and if she had been single would have cheerfully married one of the three sons, but it was one of these things which have to be said. The tea was smoked.

When we were leaving the light had shifted a little on the doorway, and the tide of shadow, flowing through all its channels, brought the whole thing to life again. We didn't go to Castle-comer but down the river valley where the trees dripped buckets of golden light on roadways between high demesne walls. Bagenalstown proved to be another comfortable river town with mills, a church in the shape of a Greek temple and rows of charming houses. In the pub we heard of a local merchant who had just died and left his fortune to provide dowries for respectable Catholic girls from the neighbourhood. It sounded just like what Bagenalstown looked, and we decided he couldn't have been some counter-jumper who had married the master's daughter but one of 'the old decent, established, respectable shopkeepers' admired by the man in Killeshin.

# 5

FROM the moment we put our foot inside the hotel in Kilkenny we felt we were not only in a different town but in a different world. It isn't an easy sort of world to describe. Every inch of hall and stair was covered with the old browns and blues of 'Spy' cartoons. There were Parnell and Michael Davitt; there Tim Healy, 'that mean-souled little man' as old John Burns called him, and not far away old John himself, in what might have been the same reefer jacket he wore when I saw him last on the terrace of the National Liberal Club.

From our bedroom window it was much the same. There was a sea of old roofs and a row of towers ranged against the sky in the rainy light: the modern Catholic cathedral, so bespiked with pinnacles and bedaubed with buttresses which streamed down its honest face like tallow from a dripping candle, that it once and for all reminded me of Good King Wenceslas with his crown and hoary locks; the modest battlemented tower of the mediaeval cathedral scarcely rising above the line of its roofs; the gay, crack-brained, white wooden tower of the eighteenth-century Tholsel, and a seedy lantern-jawed Victorian tower which looked for all the world like a street preacher. In Ireland you never know what you're missing until you find it by accident; it is tradition, the sense of the past, like a great feather-bed that your cramped and aching fancies can stretch themselves in.

Perhaps it isn't much of a past; it isn't, God knows, what you could ever call a well-preserved one, but it is a past, and in a queer way it seems to give the people who pass by you in the street an extra dimension. They seem to be just the slightest degree more substantial than the shadows you meet in towns in the west of Ireland. It is the same old phantasmagoria which fades in the same old way, but the shadows perform their parts with rather more conviction. As we went down the town our eyes strayed to a couple of Tudor chimney-pots, and we suddenly realised that the Woolworths we were looking at wasn't like any other Woolworths in the world because its glaring red front was set in an Elizabethan town house, its stone front cemented up for fear you mightn't think it sufficiently modern. A little farther down was an old furniture store which on closer examination proved to be an Elizabethan inn. Over the bridge in the ruins of St. John's, the loveliest of Kilkenny's Early English churches, the pigeons stormed furiously from the joist hollows, and the patient armoured figures on the fifteenth-century tombs turned their obliterated features to the open sky. Nobody had thought them worth taking in out of the rain.

We returned and went up the High Street, dodging down every old laneway that promised some surprise. We saw another Elizabethan gable, and pushing in the gate found ourselves in the courtyard of a fine Tudor house. We poked our way into an old almshouse, and when I asked who lived there a woman coming down the stairs replied, 'Only a few poor desolate women,' and in a strange way that lovely word with its echo of Tudor latinity rang through my ears for the rest of the evening ' as in wild earth a Grecian vase '.

In the Black Abbey, or as much as has been preserved of it, there were some decorated windows with good tracery and cusps — a very unusual feature in Ireland where only Early English and Georgian are consistently good — and it made us feel that not only had Kilkenny a tradition, but that it was a central tradition ; a tradition which did not slip into provincialism. From that we went by other lanes across the High Street to the chancel of the Franciscan Abbey. That is all that remains ; the rest is a brewery, and the apples from the neighbouring orchard were pushing their way through the tall lancets ; but the Atalantes, the fat old gentlemen and fashionable ladies who supported the arches of the tower, were full of light-hearted mediaeval fancy.

As we emerged from the brewery we caught an unforgettable view. The low painted shops of Irishtown outside the city walls drew together, and then closed in almost entirely, leaving nothing but a narrow laneway, stepped and arched, with a glimpse of coats of arms set in the wall, while above, the battlemented length of the cathedral, like an old battleship with its quatrefoil porthole clerestory and blue-grey colouring, bridged the sunken channel of the street with high roofs and massive tower. The tower itself might have been the bridge of the ship, for it rose scarcely a man's height above the roofs, and squatted above the crossing like an old bulldog guarding a heap of clothes.

On the low hill above town and river we seemed to feel freer and lighter. The west door was carved with little floating angel figures, very different from the stiff figures that followed the first phase of Norman conquest, and inside the door, cemented into the pavement where you might fail to notice them, were a few fragments of early incised tombs — a substitute for brasses. Two fragments in particular were enchanting with their flowing drapery and the sensuous drawing of opened palms. I seemed to catch the sniff of hawthorn in the May Night of the early fourteenth century ; an echo of Chaucer, Dafydd Ap Gwilym and the French songs which the young clerks of Kilkenny seren-aded their girls with in the dark laneways at night, and which the priests denounced —

*Heu, hélas, paramour*
*Qui me mist en tant doulour—*

It even got into Irish, but it didn't get very far. A genera-tion later that stone-cutter's son or apprentice was doing very different incised tombs, all in straight lines, and by the time you got to the fifteenth-century O'Tunny tombs in the transept the game was up. The effigies were traditional in their dignity, but the apostles in their panels were stiff, bewigged and goggle-eyed. Sculpture was returning to pattern. 'Life is but a shadda and man a dhrame,' as the old fellow in Bantry told us. 'The flowers is fading and we'll soon be fading ourselves,' as the little girl of fourteen in Glengarriffe piously added.

The cathedral was beautiful but there is very little I can say about the castle. Apart from the fine Georgian front which faces the row of Georgian houses at the end of the High Street, it looks, to my uninstructed eye, as if it had been entirely restored for a royal visit about the year 1910, primarily with a view to how it would appear when reflected in the river by the bridge. I never knew how much I disliked pictures until I had the opportunity of examining the picture gallery, and the only things of which I have carried away a memory are the fine over-mantel and the oak panelling, removed some years ago from the manor-house at Carrick-on-Suir.

Yet I hesitate to criticise it. The shabbiness of Irish life has turned us all into introverts ; from Swift's day to Yeats' there have been few Irishmen who knew how to use their eyes. I feel that love must be a little finer and intenser with a cathedral, a castle or a Tudor courtyard to echo its whispers in the dusk. Could it be that the shadows of out-of-works lolling against the pillars of the Tholsel were not a shade deeper than those of Cavan men ? Kilkenny was so different to every Irish town that I felt the people must be different too.

Now 'different' wasn't exactly the word that Angélique used when I stumbled across her in town the next morning. Angélique was gay, and witty and intelligent, and I felt sure she would be bound to know.

'The Kilkenny people ?' she exclaimed aghast. 'Oh, they're *awful* !'

'How are they awful ?' I asked.

'Oh, they're terrible,' she said. 'They don't know or care what goes on in the rest of the world. The very morning of Munich I talked to a woman in this very street, and she asked me who was Chamberlain. Could you believe that ?'

I could. I had been to see a local antiquarian to find out something about those incised tombs. He was a publican, and in his rooms above the pub he had a very fine collection of books and prints dealing not only with Kilkenny but with the neighbouring counties as well. He hadn't unfortunately seen the cathedral !

' But you have only to look at the big business of the town,' cried Angélique. ' There's hardly a single big shop that's owned by a Kilkenny man. Even the newspaper is run by a Kerry man. And they have no social life at all.'

' Is it possible ? ' I cried.

' Listen, my dear boy,' she said vivaciously, ' the only time one Kilkenny man gets into another Kilkenny man's house is when he's dead. You can't very well stop him then, and instead of saying " Poor Johnny is failing " as they'd say anywhere else, all you ever hear is " We'll soon get a look." '

I took careful note of everything Angélique told me, but I also took note of the fact that Angélique was a Cork woman, and the very next night I happened to be having a drink with a Tipperary officer who assured me on his word of honour that nobody ever got into the house of a Cork man, living or dead. Likewise ' the town of Naas is a horrid place ' ; likewise

> Goodbye Knockanure, so starved and so poor,
> And your church without a steeple ;
> With bitches and whores hanging over half-doors,
> Making fun of respectable people.

That night, the rain set in early. Célimène went off to bed with a book. Géronte, Orgon and I decided to go out and look for a drink. We came upon a nice-looking pub in the main street not far from the hotel as the toper flies. The shop was in darkness but the bar behind was lit up and illuminated the well-stocked shelves. But when we tried it we found the door was locked. It was still hours before closing time and the door was locked !

Géronte knocked, first discreetly, then indignantly, but no one answered. We stood on tiptoe and through the window distinctly saw figures before the counter at the back of the shop. It drove us frantic. At the least hint of real injustice wrath makes me magnificent, and while Géronte, who is made of softer stuff, modulated his solo on the knocker to tones of tender remonstrance, I pushed my way in the house door, and found myself in a hall with a full-length print of Dan O'Connell. At any other time I should probably have noticed that the print was good and wondered how it got there, but the rage was still blinding me, so I opened the door into the shop and found the shopkeeper and his wife leaning on the counter, while a Civic Guard and his friend were drinking at the bar behind.

They were all perfectly amiable. Now that we had forced our way in they accepted us as an act of God, and we felt that we had won our point, so by way of explanation the shopkeeper told us that his mother had always kept open until ten. As for himself, he never could see any reason for working such long hours, so he closed at six. It sounded perfectly reasonable as he said it ; the drink was good ; the company was good, and everybody was friendly but the parrot. She hated us. She was perched on a brass rail that ran along the wall of the shop, and she looked at me with such a fixation of malice that the lady of the house put her back in her cage, where she immediately tried to make herself sick by rocking herself violently to and fro. It was only then it began to dawn on me that there was anything unusual about the pub. The shut door wasn't Irish, no matter how reasonable it might seem, or the print of Dan O'Connell, or the parrot, or the bar itself which was a perfect little museum of pewter and copper, Toby Jugs and cut glass. There was a Penal Cross, a row of military medals and, of course, the inevitable ' Spy ' cartoons. It was tradition again. It might have been a little bar in the Cotswolds where the neighbours gather at night to discuss the news. I looked at the shelves. They were filled with wines which I had thought vanished from these islands.

Seeing that we liked his treasures, the shopkeeper brought out more of them. I couldn't say whether they were good or valuable or anything else ; all I noted with interest was that they were there at all. There were two decanters inscribed ' Outward Bound ' and ' Homeward Bound ', identical except

33

as to the stoppers, and any little difficulty about replacing these would be sufficient to indicate to the drinker that it was time he gave up. There was an octave of Cork glass; a South American dice with twelve faces and a copy of the *Freeman's Journal* for April 1883, containing a report of the trial of Tim Kelly for his part in the Phoenix Park assassinations.

'Ah, yes,' said the publican with a smile, 'the dealers didn't get much out of Kilkenny. I don't believe there's a farmhouse in the county but has something in it. I know one where they have O'Connell's duelling pistol — the one he killed d'Esterre with. That's supposed to be in his own house at Darrynane, but it isn't. It's in Kilkenny. And so is Countess Marcievicz' revolver.'

'And what about the man in Rosehill with all the glass?' said his wife.

'Just so,' he agreed. 'Thousands of pounds worth of Cork and Waterford glass.'

'And Father —,' she went on. 'Sure, you couldn't get under his bed with all the Irish silver.'

I began to see that there might be some reason for a Kilkenny man's saying 'We'll soon get a look.' At any rate there would probably be something to look at. Then the shopkeeper told us how his mother, in a fit of feminine weakness, had once parted with a decanter to a Jew for some fabulous sum. She had realised that the Jew needed the decanter badly and screwed him up to offer four times his original price. As he went out the exasperated little Jew got his revenge on her. 'I'll sell it again for three times that,' he said. That lesson had stuck in the shopkeeper's mind, and as he tinkled the ray and fah of the Cork glass, I had the feeling that no Jew would ever get much out of him.

As we hurried back through the rain past the Georgian front of the castle, the town seemed to be lit up for me. It had lost a lot; more than it could afford; but inside the Tudor and Georgian houses people still held on to things because they were old and good. Only Géronte was a bit uneasy in his mind. Late that night he came to our room to look for the *Irish Times*.

'What the hell do you want the *Irish Times* for at this hour of night?' I grumbled.

'To read the Social and Personal,' said Géronte. 'I don't believe there's a paper in this bloody town later than 1883.'

## 6

GOWRAN with its dark woods and pale-grey tower had attracted us from the Kilkenny road, so we returned that way. It was raining. The pub was deep in the shadowy cavern of the store, and a big mirror, placed in a slant very high up the wall, turned the three of us into a grand picture, like Rembrandt as to colouring and chiaroscuro, and a Russian film as to angle. But it didn't dry our wet clothes.

The ruined church was a fine bit of Early English in the lucid Kilkenny manner, with slender shafts and delicately carved caps and trefoil-headed windows finely moulded. It would make a magnificent parish church, for it is comparatively unspoiled except for the chancel where the local Protestants have built their own little horror. But at least they have given shelter to some of the carved tombs, and we spent a half-hour inside puzzling ourselves about why on earth all the Irish tomb-makers carved the effigy as if it were sinking back into the surface of the tomb.

We rejoined the Barrow at the pretty little village of Borris, where the Georgian cottages have pointed arches to their doors, by way of obeisance to the Gothic gateway of the MacMurrough Kavanagh estate which faces them. The MacMurrough Kavanaghs were once Princes of Leinster, and as we were passing we heard some sort of Angelus gun, which made me wonder whether it wasn't some ancient custom of Irish royal families. Was it not MacNeill of Barra who had a trumpeter ascend his tower every evening after dinner and proclaim ' Ye princes and potentates of earth, take heed ! MacNeill of Barra has dined. The rest of the world may now dine ' ?

The road wound round the estate and across the river, and a mile or two out we came to a beautiful ivied house by the road. Opposite it, framed in beeches and elms, silver and grey, and as if it were cut out of cardboard against the airy blue of the Blackstairs mountains, was a little Romanesque church, weathered to the colour of a tea-rose. It looked ravishing, but we found that it had suffered a little from Government protection, as the east wall had been remodelled as a ball-alley.

The river, smooth-flowing, broad and black, stemmed here and there by canal locks, dropped away beneath us; ahead, under the black slope of Mount Leinster, were two round wooded hills with the blue smoke of Graiguenamanagh rising straight from behind a brown scribble of branches. The river, which seemed about to leave it on one side, suddenly changed its mind and swept in a grand half-circle through the gap. It might have been some town in a picture of the Virgin and Child, or a Dürer landscape, so mediaeval was its air. We shouldn't have been surprised to see battlements and spires on the slopes, or a cavalcade with lances, dipping down the winding road that led into it.

A hearse and a party of mourners were standing outside the church gate as we entered the town. It was really nothing but a long narrow street leading to the hump-backed bridge under Mount Leinster. From the coffee-room of the little inn, which overlooked the river, we saw the trefoil design of Early English windows repeated in the woodwork of the shop across the road. That is one of the interesting things about towns with old churches; it shows why all the art of a particular period can be first rate merely because the lesser men are quite content to copy the greater until a newer model arrives.

The church looked exceedingly odd. The west gable jutted out into the street, and above it was something that looked like the tower of an eighteenth-century market-house. It might have been no more than my imagination, but I had noticed that the market-house was minus a tower. Inside the gate was a bit of wall with a Romanesque window in it. That proved to be all that was left of the aisles, and we entered the church through a doorway in the built-up arcade. This western part of the church was used as a vestibule; and a very squalid vestibule it was, bare and unplastered, with weeds in the fine clerestory windows and coloured shrines of Lourdes and the Crucifixion in the built-up arches of the southern arcade. There was a shocking stair which led to a gallery inside the church, and a tap-room screen of yellow glass shut off the last bay into a mortuary chapel. Inside was a coffin with candles burning round it.

But this portion of the church was at least unspoiled. In the church proper the architecture was scarcely recognisable. The level of the roof had been lowered; the clerestory and arcade built up, and ugly lancet windows inserted; there were ugly wooden galleries in the transepts. The arches at the crossing had disappeared, and the capitals were being used as bases for life-sized, coloured statues of the Sacred Heart and the Blessed Virgin. The chancel groining too had collapsed, and the remains of it were also being used as bases for rows of statues. As if that wasn't statuary enough to satisfy anybody, two more statues had been placed at either side of the high altar. As the Cashel people say of their parish church, 'It's no place for praying in — it's past that.'

The chancel arch was painted a bright blue, with angels carrying a scroll, and panels of the Ascension and Assumption. It all looked terribly out of proportion until you noticed that the arch had no bases, that tower and crossing and groining had all collapsed, and that the whole church was swimming eight or ten foot deep in their ruins. Eight or ten foot down among the graves the whole splendid old church was still complete with its tiled floors and stumps of arcading, carved doorways and tombs. 'Holy Mary, Mother of God, pray for us sinners,' roared an old man beside me in an access of devotion, and I felt rather sorry for the ghosts of the aristocratic Wiltshire monks who were its owners if ever they return to the scene of their earthly labours.

It wouldn't have been quite so bad if it had been an Irish foundation like its rival, Jerpoint, a few miles away. Those two great monasteries had sat for several hundred years like architectural images of Hibernia and Britannia, facing one another

across a few miles of hillside and river, and dragged out a per-
petual feud about a miserable little dependency until Henry VIII
simultaneously disposed of all three. At least the plainness of
an Irish Cistercian church is something even an Irish parish
priest can do little to spoil, but though Graiguenamanagh was
equally plain, it was plain with a difference. The arcade was
beautifully moulded; the double clerestory windows with
their slender dividing columns perfectly proportioned; every
detail you examined cried aloud the truth of old John Yeats'
saying that 'every Englishman has rich relations and every
Irishman has poor ones'.

One side of the little main street actually proved to be built
inside the monastery walls, and some of the kitchen gardens
were overlooked by the abbey kitchens. A heap of carved
stones had been built up to support the pole of a clothes-line.
In somebody's garage the chapter-house doorway shoved its
head and shoulders up out of the floor as though begging you to
give it a hand. Célimène returned from a voyage of exploration
looking very white. From behind the altar of the mortuary
chapel she had dragged out the head of a rake, a woman's stocking,
a salmon tin, a copy of the *Sunday Independent* six months old,
the wing of a goose, holly from the previous Christmas, a novel
called *Belinda*, a bit of curtain, the wrapping of a packet of
candles and a heap of discarded electric-light bulbs.

Just then a young nun came up to us smiling.

'You haven't seen the baptistery?'

'No,' said I.

'It's down here,' she said, opening a door off the south
transept. A flight of steps led down to the baptismal font, and
behind it was a beautiful Transitional doorway with elaborate
mouldings set off by shafts of blue stone. The capitals had
mostly been hacked away, but one of them remained with the
most delicate foliage. It was very Wiltshire-looking, very noble
and slightly frosty after the temperamental chaos upstairs. Down
that flight of steps was rather like being on a submarine voyage
to the drowned cathedral. You couldn't see it, but you could

feel it all round you with its masses of plain and tasteful ornament. The baptistery was dug out at the instigation of the O'Learys, a local family of shopkeepers, all with a streak of genius. As usual in Ireland where there are no models for young men and women, the genius had turned to antiquarianism. The brothers and sisters had drawn the abbey, written histories of the abbey, composed poems about the abbey. We had tea later on in Patrick O'Leary's room, among his axe-heads and tiles, carved chests and old books.

The nun mentioned some friends of hers in the town.

'They come from the same place,' she said with a smile, ' so naturally, we're great friends.'

'Naturally,' said I, assuming in my innocence that she came from some remote part of Cork or Donegal, and recollecting once more that ' the town of Naas is a horrid place '. 'You're not from these parts then ? '

'Oh, no,' she said, as if she were a little surprised at my even imagining such a thing. 'I'm a Carlow woman.'

'Oh,' I said again, trying to conceal the shock. After all Carlow town is only a half-hour's drive away. In time I re-collected the man from Killeshin. 'Carlow is a very pleasant town,' I went on, hoping to draw her out about it, and wondering whether it would be fair to tell her what the man in Killeshin thought of it.

'Oh, I'm not from the town,' she said hastily. 'I'm from ——, a little village across the border. You may have passed it on your way ? It's only a couple of miles out.'

'Oh, I see,' I said, to conceal the plain fact that I didn't, not really.

She saw that I was a little puzzled and tried in her gracious way to be helpful.

'They had to leave it,' she said, dropping her voice a little. 'You see, there was scandal.'

'A scandal ? ' I echoed, pricking up my ears at once. Scandals after all are my business.

'Yes,' she said with appropriate gravity. 'One of the boys fell in love with a Protestant lady.'

'Oh,' I said again, with a deep and knowing air, but again she must have detected my bewilderment.

'Naturally, they couldn't stay on after that,' she said.

'Of course not,' I said, as smoothly as I could, and with what I hoped was an appearance of conviction, but having, as you might say, been involved in a similar scandal myself, and being of an incurably romantic disposition, I couldn't just leave it at that. For the rest of my days I should have been haunted by the thought of what had really happened that daring young man and his Protestant young lady.

'And did he marry the Protestant?' I asked.

'Well, I couldn't tell you that,' she replied frankly. 'Of course I couldn't very well ask them.'

'No, of course you couldn't,' I said, still trying to pretend that I followed the story perfectly, though for the life of me I couldn't see how any young couple like that would find a place within the four seas of Ireland where the very dogs on the road wouldn't turn up their noses at them. 'But, surely,' I added, 'the neighbours must know.'

'I dare say they do,' she replied doubtfully. 'Of course, they mightn't remember.'

'Why?' I asked in surprise. 'Was this some time ago?'

'About a hundred and twenty years ago,' she replied.

I gave it up. If a man understood that, and all the infinite gradations of sentiment behind it, he would understand everything about Ireland. But at the same time I have a very strong suspicion that he wouldn't understand anything else.

## 7

'**D**O you think,' whispered the middle-aged man in the gaiters, leaning across the counter, 'you could let us have sasasa ?' and the rest of the sentence was lost on us.

'I will, to be sure,' said the publican. 'What is it ? Two bottles of stout ?'

'That's right,' said the customer eagerly, leaning farther over the counter than ever. 'But the way I am, I mamamama.'

The publican bent his head gravely to catch the mumbled excuse.

'Oh, that's all right,' he said.

'But my mrrrrrrrrrnnnn,' went on the impassioned confession, to which the publican bowed his head once more with an air of great patience.

'Ah, sure, it's all right,' he said.

'You know mrrrrrr ?'

'I do, I do.'

'Sesesesese,' said the middle-aged man, and then got his two bottles of stout and went and planted himself at a table. He was a man about one age with ourselves, and was wearing a pair of gaiters over his navy-blue trousers. We went and planted ourselves shamelessly beside him where we could hear the end of the conversation. He and his companion were talking very earnestly about the weather.

'Well, it turned very fine last evening, Willie,' said the man who had ordered the drinks.

'It did,' said Willie thoughtfully. 'We made a bit of hay.'

'So did we, Willie, so did we,' said the man in gaiters with great gravity.

'After three.'

'That's the time we made it too, Willie. Just after three it cleared up very nice. But between three and six this morning it looked very black entirely. That's why I put on the leggings, Willie, to save my clean clothes.'

'You had an early start,' said Willie sympathetically.

'Ah, well, Willie,' said the man in gaiters philosophically, 'no one ever died of hardship. No one ever died of hardship.'

He had a way of saying things that I envied him. They weren't very profound things perhaps, but he said them with a finality that fixed them for ever in your mind.

'The St. Mullins pilgrimage was good, I hear?' said the other.

'Well, I don't know, Willie. I couldn't say. I wasn't there myself. But I dare say it would be. The weather was very fine.'

'They must have made a lot of money in the pub.'

'They keep good drinks, Willie,' said the philosopher gravely.

'Do they?'

'They do.'

'Still, they gets great crowds.'

'Well, they do and they don't. When the day is fine they have a good pilgrimage, and when the day is wet, they haven't a good pilgrimage.'

'I dare say,' said Willie.

'That's the way I looks at it anyway, Willie. 'Tis only a day's outing, and what the hell more is anything else?'

'You'll have another drink,' said Willie, having digested this piece of philosophy.

'I might as well, Willie, I might as well. A bird never flew on one wing.'

They were getting nicely through the second bottle of stout when an old woman came in and planted herself alongside the philosopher and nodded amicably to us.

'Drink up that and come on away home,' she said peremptorily, giving the philosopher a nasty jab in the ribs with her elbow.

'Ah, you'll have one yourself, mother,' he said, making as if to order her a drink.

43

' I will not,' she said in a tone that could be heard at the other end of the bar.

' I got two sesesese,' he whispered, leaning across to her with his hand over his mouth.

' Who gave them to you ? ' she trumpeted. ' Was it Murphy? Drink up that, I tell you ! ' And she gave him another jab.

' If I had a half of whiskey through it now I could finish it easy enough,' he said with a man-of-the-world air that was completely lost on her. She gave him the third dig, went over to the counter and paid for his drinks, and then swept out with the two men trailing behind her like lambs. The publican told us admiringly that she was eighty-eight. I liked New Ross as I like almost every one of the Irish river towns. It has a rich, broad lyrical movement that has something in common with its rows of fine mill-houses, the eighteenth-century church which is now being used as a cinema, and the charming little Tholsel with the monument in the form of a broken harp in front of it.

We should have stuck to the river towns while we were at them. Instead we went back through Thomastown. Thomas-town itself is a pleasant enough little place, with the remains of another of those fine Kilkenny parish churches, but the only reason anyone really goes there is Jerpoint Abbey just beyond. You see it for almost the whole distance out, with its admirable tower covered in yellow moss, and as you draw nearer, it seems to swing round your course until it stands with its back to the road, and you suddenly emerge in the shadow of its fat, rosy Romanesque rump, with a triplet of plain round-headed windows.

It is all plain, even to its manners. The first time I arrived and proceeded up the bumpy grassy nave, the tower suddenly shied an enormous stone at me and missed me only by inches. I do not believe it was really a poltergeist representing the Board of Works. I suspect it is a way old churches have of drawing attention to their condition.

Its appearance is even plainer, and it makes a most striking contrast to the English foundation of Graiguenamanagh. The southern arcade has collapsed. The other consists of alternate square piers and columns, heavy and squat, supporting pointed arches with a round-headed clerestory very deeply splayed. The plain Romanesque triplet at the east end has given place to a tall Decorated window which has lost most of its decoration, but on the best day it ever was it must have been of a very spidery kind. Irish masons of the Decorated style never learned to keep their tracery sufficiently strong to make a firm pattern against the light. On the other hand the triplet of windows, which fills the whole west wall with its deep splay, is a vigorous, masculine bit of work. Likewise, the tower with its fine battlementing is big enough to dominate the whole group of buildings.

But these are not the important things about it. The important thing is that it represents the Hibernia to Graiguenamanagh's Brittania. True, it is a very superior sort of Hibernia which has been drilled in the austerity of the Cistercian rule. But there is something about it which you don't find at Graiguenamanagh. It has little grace but great charm. It is a charm which enables it to get away with murder. For instance, its cloisters, which date from the fifteenth-century, the worst period of Irish sculpture. It still has a number of the carved pillars, and others seem to have been looted to ornament a monument in the west wall. They represent a bishop, a knight, a lady, a St. Christopher, a dragon, and I suppose on any showing they must be reckoned as very poor. But curiously, they do not seem poor. There is even a figure of an angel at the base of the spidery east window (the other has been removed to make way for another infernal monument), which I swore to Célimène might have been carved by a Mestrovitch. I suppose it doesn't really bear the least resemblance to a Mestrovitch and that it was the wildest extravagance on my part to call it a masterpiece, but I feel quite certain I should never have made such a mistake in Graiguenamanagh. What else is that but charm?

It has at least one monument which is a little masterpiece. I have told how inside the door of Kilkenny Cathedral we discovered fragments of a few incised tombs with beautifully drawn drapery. In one of the side chapels of Jerpoint we found a complete though broken tombstone, obviously by the same hand. There was no mistaking that sensuous flowing line, with its touch of wistfulness and poetry. This one shows two knights in armour side by side, one with a mail cap, the other in a helmet with lowered visor. They were turned to one another with drawn swords, and we found ourselves wondering what their story was that they should be commemorated together like this. Were they brothers? Had they been killed in battle, or quarrelled and killed one another? I cannot guess, but we couldn't help contrasting their figures with those on one of the later apostle tombs. Boxed into their arcade were the whole twelve apostles, each with his appropriate symbol. They might be sitting or standing; you couldn't say. They all looked exactly alike, with eyes like marbles, and hair and beards like wigs, and all the sensuousness, the luminousness, of the Middle Ages had been bleached out as if some censor of the soul had abolished it by a stroke of the pen, and you saw exactly what happens to Ireland the moment she begins to separate herself from the rest of Europe and sinks back into herself. (Or so we thought. We hadn't yet seen what happens to the human form in Mayo and Galway.)

We felt very pleased with ourselves. Célimène went to the caretaker's cottage to get hot water for tea. At that hour of a summer's evening the old abbey was a sun-trap, and we sat on the remains of the southern arcade, admiring the cloister pillars. After our meal, we were so complacent that we committed the mistake we had always warned our friends against, and decided to go across country to Cashel.

## 8

WE didn't realise our mistake even when we reached Kells. Kells has the remains of one of those enormous Early English priories, half monasteries and half barracks, which you also find in Athassel. You couldn't get much idea of what the great church was like because it was hip-high in nettles and dirt. The chancel was completely walled off from the rest of the church by a concrete screen. We went to the other side and found it was a handball alley. As I happened to have a ball in my pocket we played a short game before the high altar, just to be able to say that we had played handball over carved tombs. Then we discovered that Célimène had lost her spectacles among the nettles.

But after one good detached look at the town of Callan we couldn't hide from ourselves the gravity of our own mistake. Callan qualified for the description a cattle-dealer gave us of Buttevant, 'a bad place for a cup of tea'. We did the only thing we could do under the circumstances and threw ourselves on the mercy of the police. They sent us to a comfortable little pub, decorated in green, white and yellow and photographs of executed Irish leaders.

But the evening ahead of us seemed endless. There was literally nothing you could do. On a house at the opposite side of the street was a tablet commemorating the diarist, Humphrey O'Sullivan. Humphrey, throughout the three volumes of his diary, never seemed to record anything but the weather. I now began to doubt if that was altogether his fault. Apart from the Catholic church, which was designed as a Greek temple, and the new Augustinian church which didn't resemble anything I had seen, the town had two beautiful ruined churches. One we couldn't get into because the Augustinians had sown the field with wheat and wouldn't let us have the key. The other

47

belonged to the Protestants whose own little church is contained within the chancel.

This was a really charming church with a fine gateway and an ivy-covered tower stuck on to the west front between two gables with Decorated windows. The nave doorways had some excellent carving, and, through their ornamental ironwork, we had a grand view of the dirty, painted Georgian street below us among its leaves. After one good look at the church and the main street, Célimène put on an important air and exclaimed, ' Sewing machine needles ! ' There is a certain stage of dereliction in Irish country towns which tells her exactly what commodities vanished from the rest of the country are likely to be found in it. In Virginia it was pot-scourers, and clothes pegs in Gurtnahoo. When she gets like that aesthetics are lost in her, and, while she was colloguing inside the shop, I stood sadly at the door looking up at the ivy-covered tower till it seemed as if the tower were looking down at me. It struck me with great force as I looked up and down the street that it and I were the only civilised things in it — I fear my head had been turned by the beauty of the Jerpoint tomb.

' What the hell brought us to this hole ? ' I asked aloud.

' It's all very well for you,' the tower replied unexpectedly. ' You can get out of it in the morning, but I have to stay on here.'

' Congregations bad ? ' I asked.

' Rotten,' said the tower. ' The Church of Ireland is going to the devil. All the decent people seem to be leaving the country.'

' I know,' said I. ' And as the woman in Myshall told us, " Everybody can be done without, but at the same time they're missed." '

' For God's sake did you see what the other fellows are after building round the corner ? ' asked the tower, referring, I knew, to the Augustinian church.

' We did glance in,' I said cautiously, for as an agnostic I dislike getting mixed up in sectarian disputes.

' And the grand old abbey church behind that they've let go to rack and ruin,' sighed the tower.

' We didn't see that,' said I. ' The monks have the place sown with wheat.'

' Talking about wheat,' said the tower, ' couldn't you do something about this ivy ? '

' I have the hands cut off myself already, pulling down ivy,' I explained apologetically. ' Of course, I could write to the Board of Works for you.'

' Board of Works ! Board of Works ! ' snorted the tower. ' Isn't it they have me the way I am ? I don't know what your politics are, young man, but I say this country has no future. No future ! '

Just then the shop door opened and Célimène came out with the eyes popping from her head.

' Got them ! ' she exclaimed with fierce glee.

The tower, I thought, looked after us a little enviously. After all it isn't entirely alone, and the two towers could exchange some interesting impressions at night across the river. I find it hard to believe they don't, but sectarianism in Ireland assumes extraordinary forms.

I was never so glad to get out of any place as Callan, but I had a bad conscience about it, for at the bend of the road I had the feeling that the tower had turned its stiff old neck and was looking after us reproachfully. If only it could reach a pub it would probably drink itself to death. But the country got worse instead of better. We stopped at a cross-roads to drink from a pump, and saw a boarded-up public-house with a ruined dwelling-house beside it, and remembered that in a five-mile spin we hadn't seen as much as one child's face. It looked like a countryside which had once had a terrible fright and never recovered from it.

At the top of a fine hill overlooking Slievenamon we came to a decrepit village with a few miserable shops and a number of condemned cottages. In the public-house there was an intelligent middle-aged woman who was full of interest in us and sympathised with us on the hill.

' Oh,' she sighed, ' 'tis often I cursed it. When I was younger

I used to cycle to Kilkenny to do my shopping.'

'To Kilkenny?' cried Célimène in astonishment. 'But that's a terrible distance!'

'Ah, but Kilkenny is a fine town,' she said fondly. 'There are grand shops in Kilkenny.'

'But wouldn't Thurles be just as good?' I asked.

'Thurles?' she exclaimed contemptuously. 'Thurles is only a market town compared to it. Waterford is a fine town too,' she continued with a sigh. 'I used to work in Waterford.'

'Then you're not from these parts?' said I.

'No, I'm a Kilkenny woman. And Tramore,' she continued eagerly. 'Do you know Tramore? Isn't it grand there in summer with all the crowds of the world at the seaside? And the quays in Waterford.'

'There was an old sailor in Youghal,' said I, 'who used to say, "By goggy, the quays of Waterford and the square of Dungarvan licks the whole world for beauty."'

'Oh, yes,' she agreed warmly, 'Dungarvan is grand,' and at that I gave her up, for when the heart grows tired the imagination begins to picture places with all the bright colours of an old picture-book, and it would take the imagination to make anything of Dungarvan. 'I worked in Clonmel too,' she continued, ticking off another bead on her rosary of recollection, and you could feel the ache of longing in her for the crowds and talk of even the most miserable of Irish towns, and it seemed to me that all Ireland was introverted in that way, and that it had struck us particularly here merely because it was a backwater of a backwater. Célimène felt it more than I did, and her voice when she spoke was full of sympathy.

'I don't suppose you see many visitors here?' she said.

'Ah, no, then,' said the woman with a toss of her head. 'Of an odd time before the war you might see a couple of English hikers, or a commercial traveller might come and stop the night. But we have no conveniences. There's no water in the village.'

'A wonder you ever settled here at all,' said I.

'Ah, musha,' she said, 'when you marry ——' and didn't finish the sentence, but her eyes finished it for her, straying as before through the open door to the ramshackle village and the bare hillside.

The instructions she gave us for reaching the next town were very explicit, too explicit, for it was clear that since she had given up shopping in Kilkenny she had got to know the other road so well that she loathed every yard of it. And as we went on, no further away than the top of the next ridge, we saw what looked like a mine-shaft against the sky. Opposite it was a fine house and shop with a big garage attached, and a man was leaning on the pillar of the gate in his shirt-sleeves. He was a fine-looking man, with a high colour and a little grey moustache. We stopped to pass the time of day, and asked him about the shaft.

'That's a coal mine,' he said, studying our features closely.

'I didn't know there were coal mines here,' said I.

'Nor a lot of others don't know it either,' he replied grimly, as though he looked on it as a grievance.

'Is it used at all now?' I asked.

'Only by the locals,' he replied. 'Would ye care to see the coal?' he asked with new interest.

'Surely we would,' said I.

He brought us into the garage, showed us a great heap of excellent coal, and explained how the local men collected it by hacking away the props of the old workings. You could see that the processes of mining had a real fascination for him. He was a superior type of man, with the extraverted intelligence you so rarely meet in Ireland. My eye was caught by a dismantled omnibus behind him.

'There you are,' he said angrily, picking up a lump of coal. 'They spent thousands, prospecting; they had engineers all over the country, looking for coal, but none of them ever came here or asked those that could have told them. That's as good as any coal you'll find in Wales.'

'Why?' asked Célimène quickly. 'Do you know Wales?'

'I do,' he replied. Cardiff, Tonypandy, Merthyr Tydfil — I was all over the shop there.'

'Ah,' I said, suddenly understanding the extravert streak in him, ' you spent some time out of the country ? '

'I did,' he replied. 'I was for years in America.'

'Mining ? ' I asked.

'No, I was a policeman.'

That explained it. I could see him, an intelligent country lad in the industrial districts of Wales and America, remembering his native place and the precious coal in it ; planning when he had saved a bit to go back and have a share in its development. He had the mind of a business man or an engineer, and I began to understand what the fine house and shop and garage were doing in that deserted corner of Ireland.

'And you came back after all ? ' I said.

'Ay,' he replied with a flash of bitterness, ' more fool I was ! I built this house and shop. I bought that bus you see there. It was very useful for taking the people in and out of town. Then they clapped a tax of seventy pounds a year on it. It ruined me. Seventeen hundred pounds I lost by it. 'Tis a rotten country and the gang that runs it. When we had the English we were well off.'

I was glad to leave him and push on. I shall never forget the picture of him in shirt-sleeves at the gate ; himself and the woman, she with her loneliness, he with his frustration, symbols of all the inhabitants of a dying countryside.

## 9

CIVILISATION in Ireland is a relative affair. Every mile we cycled downhill towards the valley of the Suir and the main road from Dublin brought us a fresh sense of liberation. We were dropping mile by mile into the great plain of Tipperary which reaches from Keeper and the Slieve Blooms in the north to the Galtees and Comeraghs in the south.

It was drawing on to evening. To the east was the slumped hulk of Slievenamon like a sleepy old dog, and the gapped peaks of the Waterford mountains below it. As the evening drew on, a semicircle of cloud gathered from the west over the mouth of the Shannon, and hauled screens of shadow across their painted sides. Farther west the Galtees were a low black rampart with the silver levers of the sun poised above them.

Then came Cashel! For one moment as we cycled down Friars' Street — to be precise, outside the Catholic church, which, according to the local joke, is no place for praying in — 'tis past that '— ' the great vision of the guarded mount ' stood directly poised on the chimney-pots of the gay painted street. Below everything was Georgian ; shadowed, solid, decorous and domestic to the last degree, and above, each outline from the lifted finger-tip of the belfry to the toy towers of Cormac's Chapel was remote, romantic and insubstantial. Even the smoke from the chimney-pots had more body.

It was all grey, the cathedral with its angle tower, the belfry with its conical cap, even the steep flagged roof of Cormac's Chapel ; a pure, pearly, translucent grey which seemed to float and melt into the evening sky, as though it were in another dimension ; an Irish Olympus. Beneath it the blessed main road from Cork to Dublin ran through the clean bright street with its charming fanlights and splendid Georgian Deanery ; in Ryan's Hotel there were parish priests and cattle dealers, one more immortal-looking than the next, scoffing bacon and eggs under the print of Lady Butler's 'Lone Hussar'. The town seemed made of the very stuff of eternity while the spectral mass of buildings above it, with its thousand years of history on its head, seemed only some trick of the light, a phantasmagoria formed of the smoke from the chimney-pots; a mirage which would vanish if you turned away your head.

The immense plain with its distant bellowing of cattle was still full of honey-coloured light when we made our way up the Rock. Mounting the steps was like mounting into history. Below us in the town, so close we could nearly have chucked stones into them, were the Dominican and Cistercian abbeys. Alone among the encircling mountain groups the Galtees had changed. For hours they had stood thunder-black on the edge of the sky with the silver levers of the sun poised above them. Now, the silver levers driven home, the planes of the mountain burst asunder, they lay all open like flowers, in great petals of gold and blue.

Before us, behind a shattered twelfth-century cross supporting itself on a crutch, was the full length of the cathedral, the west end turned into a castle, shattered on top and with a glimpse of the arch supporting the fourth storey, the transepts with angle buttresses and canopied shrines, the tall lancets half built up to save the price of glazing. Cormac's Chapel, a little tender by the Gothic hull of the cathedral, was anchored beside the choir. Cormac MacCarthy, King of South Munster in the beginning of the twelfth century, built it in the vain hope of giving his country a European outlook, and nothing else in Ireland bears any resemblance to it; an exquisite, elaborate model of a Norman church, dropped on a bare rock in the middle of Ireland, with twin towers and arcading, corbel-table and apse and barrel-vaulted roof.

Inside, its dripping walls were like a cave. The only real light came through the barred gate and the barred windows above it which were broken through in Tudor times and should have been closed up long since; but we are a poor, unfortunate people, God help us ; the English destroyed all our industries, and electric light is shocking expensive, so the rain is still beating through them and has eaten away the beautiful carved heads on the capitals beneath the vaulting and coated the north wall with a thick layer of green, phosphorescent slime through which you can barely discern the diamonds and lozenges of the arcading. The same green sub-aqueous light was reflected from the ruin of the fine sarcophagus under the west window, and through the deep gloom there was a faint, echoing glow from the red sandstone of the chancel arch with its horseshoe of pale masks.

This was European art with a vengeance. In the heads on the capitals, the hair, swept clean off the forehead, blew out like the hair of a Valkyrie ; the nose, bitten in by a rough tool, was crossed by fierce lines which swirled about the glaring eyeballs ; the beard, deeply under-cut to straddle the coign, revealed a snarl. There was nothing timid or over-decorative about the stone-cutting at any rate.

I suppose there isn't another country in Europe which would permit such a masterpiece to remain in such a condition, but Cormac MacCarthy and his friends were probably the last European-minded Irishmen in positions of authority. All we know of Cormac makes him a most attractive figure. In that age of violence he committed only one murder (there is one person we all want to murder) and had only one mistress (few of us can do with less). The twelfth-century 'Vision of Tnugdael', written by one who knew his little court, condemns him to one hour of Purgatory out of the twenty-four to atone for these offences. The rest of the time he is attended not by his own courtiers but by the artists and poor people he had served in life. St. Malachy was his friend, and St. Bernard of Clairvaux, who took a poor view of the little kingships, writes of him with respect.

His friends were a very gallant group of laymen and priests from Ulster and Munster who very nearly succeeded in re-organising Ireland as a European state immediately before the Norman invasions beat it flat. The dramatic story of their attempt has been told in Dean Lawlor's great edition of St. Bernard's *Life of Malachy*, though as neither Dean Lawlor nor Edmund Curtis seems to have grasped fully the interdependence of ecclesiastical and political history in twelfth-century Ireland, the *Life of Malachy* needs to be read with Curtis' *Mediaeval Ireland*.

It all began with the O'Briens, the most European-minded of the Irish royal families. Politically the O'Briens were on the decline before the O'Connors of Connaught and the O'Neills of Ulster, but they were the first to realise how they could re-establish themselves by the aid of the Church. Their difficulty was that there was no organised Church, merely a number of tribal monastic foundations, controlled by stewards appointed by the reigning families. The Gaelic mind abhorred novelty, and to attack this old system directly would have invited disaster. Murtagh O'Brien began by introducing two English-trained bishops into the Danish sees of Waterford (1096) and Limerick (1105). A year after the latter appointment a young man called Ceallach who was sympathetic to the reform movement, finding himself chosen steward of the primatial Church in Armagh, took holy orders and rode south to the O'Brien country to have himself consecrated Bishop by the two Roman bishops there.

This, which was either an extraordinary bit of luck or more probably a brilliant intrigue on the part of Murtagh, who had made friends amongst the monks of Armagh, put the reformers in an unassailable legal position, because Ceallach, now Bishop of Armagh, was *ipso facto* Primate of Ireland. He in turn made the Bishop of Waterford Archbishop of Cashel. With this rudimentary organisation they summoned in 1110 a synod for which the Bishop of Limerick, a canonist, drew up a scheme of diocesan organisation to take the place of the old monastic one.

This was admirable but it excluded Connacht from any position of authority. Murtagh O'Brien died, and his widow married Turlough O'Connor, King of Connacht. Turlough knew what was afoot. He split the O'Brien kingdom into two and established Cormac's father as King of South Munster. When the Cross of Cong was made in 1123, the steward of

Cong, O'Duffy, was described on it as 'Bishop of Connacht', proof enough that Connacht was not going to allow the pallia to be divided in the way the reformers wished. Cormac's father died, and he was chosen as King. It did not suit Turlough O'Connor to have a man sympathetic to reform on the throne — Cormac had been educated at Lismore where he had become friendly with Ceallach's disciple, St. Malachy — so a Connacht fleet landed in Cork, drove Cormac out and established one of his relatives in his place. Cormac went back to Lismore with the intention of becoming a priest.

This was not at all what the Roman bishops wanted. Malachy was sent to persuade his old friend to form an alliance with Conor O'Brien, King of North Munster, who was also sympathetic to the reform movement, and between them the two men overthrew the puppet government of the O'Connors and Cormac was King again.

Then it was Malachy's turn. In 1125 Donnchadh O'Carroll, one of the finest figures in the reform, became Prince of Oriel. By another clever bit of intrigue Malachy was made Bishop of Clogher, but the O'Neills were even less sympathetic than the O'Connors and he was promptly driven out, taking refuge with Donnchadh who built him a monastery in Newry. Malachy, who, because of his friendship with St. Bernard, was the only reformer to secure European recognition, is really the least interesting of the group. He was a very ambiguous figure, half European churchman, half Irish hermit.

Then Ceallach felt death coming on. He knew that before he was in his grave his family would appoint another steward, and Armagh and its cathedral, which he had re-roofed after a hundred and fifty years during which it had remained a ruin, would again pass back to the old tribal system. He knew too that no one but an Ulsterman could take his place. Once more in 1128 or 1129 he rode south to the O'Brien country. It was probably on this last journey — certainly not very many months before — that his party was attacked by O'Connor's ruffianly lieutenant, O'Rourke, and a number of them murdered, including

a little acolyte. On his death-bed in Co. Limerick he made a
will leaving the primacy to Malachy — but pledging the two
kings of Munster to install him at the point of the sword !

This is one of the most astonishing and moving episodes in
Irish history. Politically, its purpose is perfectly clear. Donnchadh O'Carroll, established on the borders of the O'Neill
country, was sympathetic, but his tiny forces could not hope to
beat the O'Neills alone. If a Munster army attacked the O'Neills
on the flank and laid their country waste it would leave his
hands free. But from the traditional Irish point of view it was
treachery of the worst kind ; — an appeal by an Ulsterman for a
foreign army to invade his country in the interests of the Church.
If Malachy had been a big enough man to realise it this dramatic
will, which once and for all cut clean across the artificial
boundaries of the country, could have been a death-blow to
the little kingdoms and the tribal monasteries. But Malachy
was always rather the Irish hermit than the European ecclesiastic ;
all he foresaw was the certainty of civil war, and he refused to
leave his monastery.

Years passed. As Ceallach had foreseen, another steward
was appointed ; then he in turn died, and with the election of
his successor, Ceallach's uncle, the Roman bishops saw that the
primacy was becoming a dead letter once more. In 1133 the
mock abbot made a visitation of the O'Neill country and received
tribute from them. Then followed another episode almost
as dramatic as the previous ones. The Bishop of Limerick was
Papal Legate, and he and the other bishops threatened Malachy
with excommunication. In face of this, Malachy agreed to
accept the terms of Ceallach's will, but with a proviso which
was to work endless mischief, that, once the principle was
established, he should be permitted to retire. At first he did not
attempt to occupy Armagh, but lived outside it with an armed
guard, obviously protected by Donnchadh O'Carroll who was
still not in a position to move. Then in 1134, the same year
that saw the completion of Cormac's Chapel — the standard of
the reform movement — the Munster army moved up through

Connacht, fighting their way towards Armagh from the opposite direction and burning the family church of the O'Neills at Maghera on their way. (The O'Neills rebuilt it but *not* in the Romanesque style.) When Malachy was in a position to occupy the town the people hooted him. Several attempts were made to murder him, but he stood his ground.

At last, some of the O'Hagans who were lying in wait for him were struck by lightning (it was one of the minor ironies of the position that Ivar O'Hagan, Malachy's tutor, was himself a reformer). Then the O'Neills came to terms. It was agreed that they should recognise Malachy as Primate but that he should withdraw in favour of Giolla Mac Liaigh, abbot of the O'Neill monastery in Derry. Obviously, Derry, though only a couple of miles from the O'Neill palace of Aileach, had already accepted the Roman obedience. The O'Neills had attempted to burn it out in 1126, but the monks and townspeople had fought them off and killed their king. They were more successful in their next attempt. But though the election was in some ways a victory for the reform movement and established in Armagh the principle of clerical control of Church property, it also re-established the tribal organisation of the Catholic Church in Ireland, which in many places went on uninterruptedly into Tudor times.

Obviously, the compromise staggered the Munster clerics. From this on they practically ceased to attend synods presided over by Giolla Mac Liaigh and dominated alternately by O'Connors or O'Neills, whichever happened for the moment to be on top. Munster almost voted itself out of the rest of Ireland, and went over, Church and State, to the Normans on their arrival. It was the only course which seemed to promise the bringing of the entire country within the Roman obedience. The final blow was the distribution of the pallia. At the Synod of Kells in 1152, Dublin (which being subject to Canterbury and half Danish always dissociated itself from the reform) received one ; Connacht, because of the new supremacy of the O'Connors, another. Tuam, Armagh, Cashel, Dublin —

after fifty years of desperate struggle the only result of the reform movement was to establish four provincial churches instead of one in which north and south were united. The Cistercians, magnificently backed by Donnchadh O'Carroll, still tried to maintain a sort of unity, but with very indifferent results. Their first great foundations were established within Donnchadh's territory where, while that fine soldier lived, they were absolutely secure ; they spread through Leinster, the territory of Diarmuid MacMurrough, and had, of course, a great number of houses about Cork and Limerick. With the aid of the MacDermotts they established one foundation in Connacht, and much later Cahal O'Connor Redhand allowed them another near Tuam. The O'Neills never allowed them to establish a single house within their territory. It is quite clear that until the end of the twelfth century they were still under suspicion among the Irish kingeens. Irish Romanesque and Transitional architecture, whose origins and dates have excited the wildest guesses among antiquarians, become comparatively easy to understand if you mark their positions on a map showing the old political boundaries.

WITH the usual difficulty of mediaeval masons in setting out a large church, the builders of the cathedral found as they proceeded that they had to cut through Cormac's Chapel. The great north porch, overshadowed by the cathedral wall, is partly swallowed up in it, and the west windows of the chapel emerge mysteriously in the cathedral transept. It is a lofty aisleless building of the thirteenth century, one of the innumerable O'Brien churches; its carving stiff by comparison with the contemporary English work in Kilkenny, its clumsy chancel clerestory an afterthought. In the fifteenth century the west front was turned into a castle, which, particularly at that hour of evening, made the church gloomier and ghostlier than it need be. But in that particular century of the Irish revival, as barbarous as the twelfth but with little of its brilliance, there was every need for a castle. The Irish never really got over their childish delight in arson.

> The fury of the fire dissolves
> The frost that sheaths the tranquil eye,
>   And from his wrists the flame
>   Thaws manacles of ice

— as Hugh Maguire's bard sang in his learned way, while the Calvach O'Connor's wrote a positive hymn to arson —

> Our lads stay to toast their shins
>   Till the castle's ours,
> Never bandage wounds till fire
>   Crackles through the towers;
> They burned Cashel, they burned Thurles—
>   Best of stormy marches;
> Any market day in Limerick
>   They can crack the arches;
> Any day can burn Kildare;
>   Naas they've burned already.

The miracle is that there is any architecture left, and that what there is of it, considering the slender chance of its survival, is so good.

Mr. Minogue, the caretaker, was showing round a party of visitors, one of whom was a nun, and, tempering the wind to the shorn lamb, explained that the fertility goddess, without whom no Irish church would be complete, was really a wind fairy. He was also, I thought, rather diffident about telling the full story of Myler Magrath whose tomb is in the chancel. Of course, Myler himself was not exactly frank. 'The scaldpriest', as the Tudors called him, began life as a Franciscan monk and seems to have ended it at the age of a hundred or so as a Franciscan monk, but in between married, became a Protestant bishop several times over, and held Protestant services for a congregation of one in the cathedral while upstairs some hunted Catholic priest said Mass for his wife and children. They were Catholics as Myler was a Protestant; 'a wife like her husband and a husband like nobody', as one Gaelic poet described Anna Magrath. She and they shared in the looted benefices, while Myler succeeded brilliantly in playing off the Pope, Queen Elizabeth, Raleigh and Hugh O'Neill against one another. In his old age they sent him an English coadjutor to help him with his congregation of one, but the coadjutor took to the bottle and had to be recalled. In extreme old age Myler, like Browning's bishop, ordered his tomb and wrote his epitaph, but by this time he was so cautious of making any decisive statement that the epitaph has been taken to mean that he isn't buried here at all.

He is one of Cashel's ghosts and not by any means the least important. There are others more violently taken off. Murrough O'Brien — Murrough of the Burnings, as they called him from his addiction to the national pastime — had a splendid outing here with his Roundhead troops. Before Myler's tomb and up the tower stairs they slaughtered the Catholics of the town. 'They broke the heads, hands and feet of the great crucifix which hung at the entrance of the quire', writes the Jesuit, Saul, in a contemporary account. 'Some, clad in the

62

sacred vestments, and walking round wearing birettas, jeeringly invited one another to Mass. Some dashed the holy images against the walls and tombs; others carried our great statue of the Blessed Virgin, ingeniously ornamented with gold, through the streets, having first chopped off the head. Others wrapped up in horse-cloth and carried away in sacks the statues of St. Patrick, St. Ignatius and the other saints (they repeatedly called them deaf and dumb). There was one who continued to jeer a smaller statue of Our Lady which he had, saying, "Mary of Ireland, where are you now? Would you like a few peas?"'

It is one of the most moving descriptions of the Roundhead desecrations, but like everything else in Ireland it has its own ambiguity. The author died as a Protestant clergyman in the selfsame diocese of Cashel. In the eighteenth century one of its bishops was Theophilus Bolton, who admired Cormac's Chapel and invited Swift down to look at it. He was succeeded by one of Swift's enemies, Price, the blockhead who courted Vanessa and whom on her deathbed she dismissed with the words 'No Price, no prayers', and a profane quotation from *The Tale of a Tub*. He is generally credited with leaving it unroofed. In the nineteenth century the east end collapsed and has stayed collapsed. The seat of the Catholic archbishop has been transferred to the atrocity at Thurles, and the great mass of buildings in which the whole history of Ireland is concentrated, abandoned by both Churches, exists only on the grudging charity of the Commissioners of Public Works.

## ❧ II ❧

CASHEL is not only good in itself, but, having a good hotel, is an excellent centre for seeing the rest of Tipperary. Fethard, Athassel Priory and Holy Cross Abbey, all worth seeing, are within a radius of ten miles through pleasant country. Fethard is the town which protested against Cromwell's midnight summons to surrender as contrary to the laws of war, and is still ' a bad town for a cup of tea '. But the ruins of its two abbeys have been partially restored, the one by the Augustinians and the other by the Protestants, which gives you some idea of what could be done by intelligent restoration to give back some of their character to these nondescript Irish towns.

But the best jaunt for a summer's morning is through the heart of the rich Cashel plain to Holy Cross and Thurles. Part of the way you find yourself cycling by the river with its old mill-house, and suddenly come upon the abbey itself with a lonesome lump of hill behind it which somehow seems to have got detached from the rest of its comrades in the Slieve Ardaghs. We went into the pub for a drink and found ourselves sitting beside an old man. We saluted him, but he didn't say ' good morning ' or ' fine day '. There was a jaunty-looking man drinking at the bar who may have been the cause of his depression. He strutted to and from the door with an important air and then paused dramatically in front of us. ' Old man,' he said, ' you're very white.' ' The cabbage isn't good till 'tis white,' replied the old man morosely.

The abbey is peculiar. To begin with, we could hardly get a picture of the church because of the ' buttresses ', great stacks of masonry heaped up about the walls inside and out and as ungainly-looking as the Decorated windows in the transept window beside them. For a time I couldn't even make out what they were doing there, until I remembered the corner buttresses of English Perpendicular, which almost look as if they were intended as shutters, to fold back. The Holy Cross buttresses seem to have been the result of some vague rumour of these goings-on, but they ruined whatever grace the twelfth-century church might have had. As we entered through the little gate in the north transept, the sunlight from the roofless nave was being reflected up into the high clustering ribs of the tower arches, while pure sunlight poured in a cascade down the grassy night stairs from the dormitory into the crossing.

That cheered us up a bit, but the interior, crammed with unsightly gravestones, cast us down again. There were fine canopied sedilia and a shrine, both of which showed the influence of not quite so contemporary English work, but the rest of the church had been rebuilt in the blowsy manner of the Irish fifteenth century, with anachronistic Decorated windows which ranged from the merely clumsy over the altar to the outstandingly God-awful in the west wall. (' The most striking feature of the exterior of the church,' said our guide-book, ' is the beautiful and unusual window tracery, that of the E. and W. windows and the south transept being especially remarkable.') You can still see traces of the plain and beautiful Romanesque windows they replaced, and if you have good eyesight, and the walls aren't too damp, you may even be able to make out traces of wall-painting in the chancel.

It made us feel again that civilisation is merely a matter of communications. Here were we with nothing but the Slieve Ardagh hills between us and Callan where Decorated work, though equally anachronistic, was still comparatively good, and already decent tracery and cusps had disappeared. Fifteenth-century work on its way across Ireland has a tendency to lose its feathers till it ends up in the remoter parts with the shocked air of a plucked goose. Holy Cross was a sort of half-way house between Dublin and the west ; between the thirteenth and the nineteenth centuries ; good but tasteless ; a Sancho Panza–Friar Tuck, honest-to-God meal of architectural pig's-cheek and cabbage, pointing the way to what Irish Catholicism became when it lost the last of its Continental refinements.

We cycled east along the edge of the Slieve Ardaghs. They stretch all the way to Kilkenny, with a great plain of bogland in front of them. Within a mile or two of the foothills we stopped for a drink at the little village of Gurtnahoo. It was, I think, the second clean village we had seen. Then and there an argument sprang up between us as to why one village should be clean and all the rest dirty. Célimène said it was wealth, and I that it was a parish priest who gave the villagers a lead. She said people in Ireland were too poor to care very much whether their homes were clean or not, and I instanced Cavan where they were dirty whether the people were poor or not. We never found out exactly why Gurtnahoo was clean, for as we entered the pub Célimène clutched me feverishly by the arm.

' Clothes pegs ! ' she hissed.

By this time I was so used to her fits of excitement that I presumed clothes pegs must be a bit of a rarity. While I ordered the beer, she deliberately sat with her back to the row of clothes pegs as if they were the last things in the world she was thinking of, and proceeded to make eyes at the young man behind the counter.

' How far is it from this to Kilcooley Abbey ? ' I asked.

' About a mile or two up the road,' he replied.

' I dare say there isn't much of it left,' said I.

' Of what ? ' he exclaimed.

' The abbey,' said I.

' The abbey ? ' he repeated with a puzzled air. ' Oh, it's all there.'

' What I mean,' said I, ' is that I suppose it's a ruin.'

' Oh, no, no,' he replied rather doubtfully. ' I wouldn't call it a ruin.'

' You don't mean it's in use ? ' I asked, wondering whether it hadn't like Fethard been partially restored as a parish church.

' Oh, yes, it is,' he replied.

' Kilcooley Abbey ? ' said I in astonishment.

' Kilcooley Abbey,' he repeated, and we looked at one another.

'Really?' said I, and for a moment I could think of nothing more to say.

'Of course,' he went on, 'it's not as important a place as it used to be.'

'Naturally not,' I said smoothly. 'But you tell me that services are still held there?'

'Services?' he echoed, as if he thought I wasn't quite right in the head. 'Of course they are. The whole place is still in working order.'

'Maybe,' I thought in a daze, 'they haven't yet heard about the dissolution of the monasteries.' Civilisation, as I say, is largely a matter of communications, and communications in Ireland are still damn bad. I had a vision of myself securing an exclusive interview with the abbot and getting his first impression of the Reformation, but then I began to get angry with myself and determined on worming out the facts.

'But how did that happen?' I asked, as if I didn't see anything particularly unusual about a Cistercian monastery still functioning a couple of miles off the main road from Cork to Dublin.

'Ah,' he said lightly, 'they still have the abbey lands, or a lot of them at any rate.'

'Oh, God!' I thought with a sickening feeling at the pit of my stomach, 'this is Berkeley Square or Pirandello or Priestley or some such literary nonsense!' I am not an intolerant man, and I have a real weakness for hymns, Catholic, Anglican or Salvation Army, but there is something in me that reacts away from the supernatural. I looked at Célimène, begging her to come to my assistance, but nothing was further from her mind at that moment than monasteries.

'I suppose you couldn't let me have a few of those clothes pegs?' she asked with a devastating smile.

'Clothes pegs?' said the young shopkeeper, brightening up at once at the mention of something familiar. 'Certainly. How many would you like?'

'Two dozen, if you can spare them,' said Célimène.

'Oh, to be sure, to be sure,' he said obligingly, and she hadn't got them safe and sound before she wanted to be off, just in case he might change his mind.

'You simply can't get them in Dublin,' she said intensely as she covered them up in the Travelling Kitchen.

'Never mind about the clothes pegs,' I snapped. Out in that clean sunlit street I couldn't possibly believe in Priestley. 'Did you notice what he said?'

'What did he say?' asked Célimène.

'That the abbey was still in use,' said I.

'He ought to know,' said Célimène warmly, as if any reflection on the shopkeeper must imply a reflection on the clothes pegs.

'How the devil could he know?' I snapped irritably, and I cycled on, still trying to think it out. Then I began to curse, for the road to the abbey had been repaired with sharp stones the size of eggs, thickly sprayed with tar. I switched on to the footpath, still thinking of the dissolution, till I suddenly came upon a trench dug across the footpath. There was nothing for it but to jump back on to the road. I did, and jumped clean into Célimène who was coming up the edge of the road a little behind me. She fell heavily and rose with her best jodhpurs covered in tar. She was angelic, as she always is before the absolutely irremediable, but contrition banished all thought of the great problem from my mind till we came to the high wall of a demesne and a ragged child coming up the road from the main gate.

'Where is Kilcooley Abbey?' I asked her.

'This is Kilcooley Abbey, sir,' she replied, pointing to the demesne wall.

'Oh, God help me, what am I to do?' cried Célimène with an anguish that came from the heart.

The infant was right. They gave us the key at the lodge, and we went up a long avenue which reminded me of my own translation of the Irish song 'Kilcash'—'your avenue needs attention'; — and to the left was the church which the shopkeeper thought I was referring to, and to the right the ruined abbey church which I was really referring to, and even from the other side of the field we could detect that it had been restored at the same time and by the same masons as Holy Cross.

It was highly fortified ; we crossed the remains of a moat, and the aisles had been torn down and the arcade built up so as to deprive attackers of easy access to the roof, and about it were the same stacks of masonry that passed in the fifteenth century for buttresses. The only door was through the cloister side, and an entrance had been rudely torn through the groining of the north transept. In the south transept, shutting off the first from the second chapel, was a high canopied screen with a beautifully moulded door surmounted by a crudely carved crucifixion. It seemed clearly to be the work of the same man who carved the fine sedilia at Holy Cross. There were sedilia by the same skilful hand, bastard Decorated windows by the same clumsy ones, and a complete apostle tomb in the chancel. There was one tomb in particular which gave me great pleasure : a plain slab incised with the portrait of an old man, an unusual and effective idea.

It must be one of the most complete examples of an Irish abbey in existence, for the cloisters too were in comparatively good condition, and there were even some of the living-rooms which still retained their ceilings, door-frames and fireplaces. And for some reason — perhaps because it is never mentioned in the guide-books and came as a complete surprise to us, or because, when we stood at the back of the high, aisleless, doorless nave and the shadow of the west wall with the tracery of a clumsy window was thrown on the round arch which supported the low, broad, shallow tower — there was no clutter of abominable gravestones to spoil the view, we were enchanted with it.

After that, nothing would do Célimène but to look at the Big House. Some glimpse through a gateway of weeds in a garden had peopled her mind with Gothic fantasies, and even when we were admiring the long, low Georgian front spoiled by nineteenth-century bay windows, she swore that at any moment a mad old lady armed with a carving knife would come and chase us down the avenue. Being of a realistic disposition, I imagined instead a bored and inquisitive colonel asking us in for a resiner (as a matter of fact, we were both wide of the mark, for even a long way from Kilcooley we found country people speaking with respect of the Ponsonbys). The neglected lawn looked down on a sleeping lake which mirrored a half-circle of dark trees and the Gothic front of what may have been a 'hermitage'. In the evening light it filled us with a ninetyish melancholy, with Verlaine's poetry and Debussy's music. Above the dark sickle of the woods there should have been a pale moon reflected in the lake. Instead, before the front door there stood a splendid oak, riven above its lowest branch and smitten magnificently to the ground.

## 12

WHEN I asked the boots in Roscrea the way to Monaincha, pronouncing it as it is spelled, he said he had never heard of it. 'Would it be Monaheensha?' he asked, and of course, Monaheensha it was, and already it began to assume an existence outside the pages of a guide-book.

Roscrea is one of the most charming of Irish towns — potentially at least. It is tossed about in choppy country of little hills which you find looking at you from the end of every street; streets of pleasant little houses with sculped-in doorways; a fine castle on the hilly main street with a magnificent Queen Anne house in stone built in the courtyard, and a Franciscan abbey with a sentimental little tower behind.

But the best thing in it is the fragment of a parish church which was abandoned at the beginning of the last century merely because the Protestant Church Sustentation Fund would advance money only for new buildings, not for the restoration of old ones. It now consists of nothing but a west wall, and it is remarkable that even this has survived, for a main road was driven clean through the monastery enclosure, isolating the belfry in a garage at the opposite side of the road.

It had poured steadily all the evening, and the wet, woodbine-coloured light was bringing out all the gold in the spongy yellow sandstone while the churchyard sulked behind in a cold, cavernous, sea-green light. It was a recollection of Cormac's Chapel; a porch set in an arcade of four arches, each with a pediment that echoed the pediment of the porch and what (before they lowered the level of the roof and tacked on the little bell-cote) must have been a high gable. It was fearfully worn, for the chalky stone laps up the rain like blotting-paper, and the saint in the pediment and the heads on the capitals had almost crumbled away; but it still had some of the elegance of Cashel, the same sense of a civilised life directing it. The exterior arches were ornamented, the inner ones plain : the variation was Irish, the symmetry European.

It is a church I have a particular affection for, because so far as I can recollect it was the first bit of architecture I looked at with pleasure. In the usual way of the tourist I had seen some of the French cathedrals and the great Italian art towns, and for all the difference it had made, I might just as well have stayed at home. And then one day, when Célimène and I were cycling from Dublin to Limerick, we arrived in the heel of the evening at Roscrea, and, suddenly turning a right-angled bend, found ourselves passing this plain little Romanesque front. We jumped off and had a good look at it, but somehow I knew from the first moment that this meant more to me than any building I had seen before. We went on to the hotel and had our supper, and Célimène went off to bed, but I returned to the little church just as the shadow had worked up to the level of the roof, and the little bell-cote seemed to float on the air, and stood there looking at it till darkness fell. I could barely remember a time when I didn't understand what people meant when they talked in poetry and music, and before I could read or write I understood the music of 'How Dear to Me the Hour when Daylight Dies' and the poetry of

> Though lost to Momonia and cold in the grave
> He returns to Kincora no more.

But at the age of thirty-five I still didn't understand how people spoke through stones and slates. I thought it must be something to do with what the guide-book referred to as 'Irish Romanesque', so we changed our direction to find more churches of the same kind, but it wasn't that ; and it wasn't until I found myself delighting in a row of little eighteenth-century houses by a river that I realised the art with which a builder erects a house so that to the memory it spells ' home '.

We left the main road and turned along a bumpy bog road with a disused distillery at the top of it, and there came to us over the ridges of it a long procession of high blue-and-orange creels, laden with turf, the heads of the little asses forced level with the shafts. It was drawing on to dusk; the fields were filled with brown rushes, and where the ground rose out of the bog to right and left there were groves of beeches, black with rain and bronzed with mast. The smell of burning turf clung like mist to the ground.

And then where the narrow road made a sudden bend overhung with beeches we came to a wicket gate in a demesne wall. It was a gate I shan't forget in a hurry because the sagging wall had pulled it awry till it looked like a mouth in a paralysed face; and quite suddenly there flashed before my mind a picture of a winter night glittering with frost and a cart with a little candle lamp, rattling home from Roscrea. There was a child sitting at the back of the cart, and as it passed the gate he drew a bit of sacking over his head because he was afraid of the ghosts.

I saw it quite plainly because I was the child on the cart, and I was terrified of the ghosts. I pulled up and said to Célimène, 'This is a place they see ghosts in' (she wrote it in her diary the same night). Now, I had no idea that the fields where the rushes were growing was once a wide lake, or that the church we were going to see stood on a one-time island called in all mediaeval documents Insula Viventium because nobody was supposed to be able to die on it, and when they got really ill, had to be sent across to the mainland. I found that out weeks after.

The only one of the island churches that remains stood on a hillock in the middle of the boglands with a wall of beeches about it; three bare cottage gables, the one that faced us touched by the woodbine-coloured light till it was one tone with the trees. A muddy lane led to the little Protestant cemetery where the graves were marked with small flat slabs of sandstone from the church roof or tiny ornaments from the Early English windows. The doorway had been restored by somebody with no eye for the tapering. I didn't realise until I started looking at English churches, which all seemed for some reason to be standing to attention, how much of the character of Irish ones depends

73

on the diminishing perspective of windows, doors, gables and towers that makes them all seem to be standing easy, legs spread, firmly based on the landscape.

Yet it still gave the church its atmosphere ; a touch of Egypt, of the hooded falcon, in the high-shouldered pilasters gripped as in a steel band by the frieze of capitals. It certainly wasn't the charming little chancel arch, woman-curved, with smooth columns, scalloped capitals and a web of smoothly-flowing superficial ornament, the colour of red bronze in the evening light, nor the thirteenth-century east window which opened on to a clump of sunlit beeches. There was a family called Birch buried inside ; one was described as a native of London.

The cold drove us away at last, the penetrating cold that comes out of half-reclaimed land. We had disturbed the haunt of some yokels who were having the time of their lives, trying to scare us by popping up over walls and through window openings. When we came out it was just as if the church were islanded again because all round us was a lake of white mist, with the lamps twinkling in the little cottages upon its banks.

We came back next morning when the sun was shining brightly and the gaily-coloured carts were clattering back to the bog, but the little church seemed to cling to its secret. One of the minor pleasures of architecture is the way in which buildings which haven't been too much looked at seem to secrete something of what they have experienced. Monaincha somehow suggested remoteness. It wasn't a place you could ever grow fond of. Perhaps it has seen too much. In the Middle Ages it had been a place of mystery. In the Penal Days it had been a place of refuge, and Catholics put off in boats at dawn from the shores around to hear Mass said by some hunted priest. Then the Birches came, drained the lake, buried their dead in the chancel and removed the church of the nuns to make decorations for their new garden. But the old church waited in its remoteness.

' The family ', said the old cattle dealer with whom we cycled on to Borris-in-Ossory, ' is now extinct.' There was nothing you could actually call regret in his tone. I guessed his business from the switch tied to the lady's bicycle he was riding in the place where the cross-bar would normally be. He was going to Borris to complete a deal, and it would not be binding without the traditional touch of ' the rod '.

He was a chirpy, light-hearted old man and a great repository of traditional topographical lore like ' wracked and wrecked like Mitchelstown ' ; ' wherever the devil is by day, he's in Cappa-white by night ' ; Carlow, ' poor but proud ' ; and Leix, ' poor, proud *and* beggarly ; kiss you and cut your throat '. (The woman in the pub in Rathdowney solemnly assured us of the exactness of the last statement, and added the further information that while the most ·respectable Tipperary man would appear on Sundays with an open neck, a Leix man wouldn't even go to the workhouse without a collar and tie on.) When we asked what he thought of Clare men he merely groaned. In fact, the only foreigners he had a good word to say for were Kerry men. ' A good Kerry man is as good a man as you'll meet.'

' And what part are ye coming from ? ' he asked.

' Monaincha,' said I.

' Monaincha ? ' he exclaimed in surprise. ' What were ye doing in Monaincha ? '

' Looking at the old church,' said I.

' Ye didn't see any ghosts ? ' he asked.

' No,' said I, but at the same time my heart gave a bit of a jump. ' Are there ghosts ? '

' The place is full of them,' he said. ' Ye didn't happen to see a little gate in a wall by the bend of the road ? '

' We did,' said I. ' Is it there the ghosts are seen ? '

' The very place,' he said. ' There's people wouldn't pass that place after dark.'

The little gate, it seemed, led to the Birches' garden, and he told us about the Birches and their distillery, and from the quiet voice in which he added ' The family is now extinct ' I had the feeling that there was a lot he had not told us about the Birches, apart from the fact that their garden still contains the carved stones of the nuns' church and a fine window from the Franciscan abbey in Roscrea.

He left us by the coffee-pot church at Borris.

'Look after the missus and mind the trams,' he shouted back at me.

## 13

STARTING off from Cashel we cycled to Golden, which was once a charming little village with a Big House and an old tower on the Suir, but the housebreakers had got there a little before us, and the Big House was now a hideous gash on the landscape with its gutted walls and stables. Why on earth any Irish government should imagine that Ireland hadn't ruins enough and that it was their duty to fill it with more, I didn't understand, but then there is a lot about Irish governments which I don't understand.

From that, we cycled by a bumpy by-road along the river into the blue range of the Galtees. The swans floated tranquilly beside the remains of one of the finest of the Early English priories which once guarded a ford of the Suir against raiders from the further side. There was a dried-up moat, a bridge and a gate-house with carved capitals that led to an enormous bawn where the monastery cattle were driven at night. The west front of the church had collapsed; in fact little remained of the nave but some stumps of the arcade, but you could imagine what the front had looked like from the screen before the chancel with its handsome moulded door and shrines. Like Cashel, it gives an appearance of great height, and in the transepts the arches of the tower had been taken off stout columns built high up in the walls, but it was so dirty and neglected that we found ourselves without heart. We used our knives to dig out an incised tomb from before the high altar, and it didn't seem to be worth it when the job was done. The most interesting parts of the building since they had suffered least were the cloisters.

We skirted the flank of the Galtees with the wind dead behind us and it blew us into a great fan of mountains through a country of orchards and wheat where the milk-churns were shining by whitewashed gateposts under overhanging boughs — lovely lyrical country, or was it the wind that made it seem so? To a cyclist there are really only two sorts of landscape, with and against the wind. I shot ahead as joyous as a yacht in a gale, to catch up with the village postman cycling home with his empty bag. He was a finely-built man with a broad, bony face and a rather quiet, thoughtful air. We passed the time of day, and he looked at my shorts and knapsacks.

'That's a good way of travelling,' he said at last.

'It is,' I agreed enthusiastically. With that wind behind me I couldn't have wished for a better.

'I did a long spin like that myself once,' he said thoughtfully.

'Did you?' I asked in surprise, for in the country it is only Englishmen who are supposed to be capable of that sort of folly. ('A very simple race,' we were told by the woman in Rathdowney.)

'I did,' said the postman. 'I cycled from this to the Junction and then on to Cork. Do you know Cork?'

'Cork?' said I. 'Why wouldn't I? Wasn't I born and reared there?'

'Is that so?' exclaimed the postman with a gleam of interest. 'Then maybe you'd know a place called Leap?'

'To be sure I do,' said I. 'Why did you ask me?'

'That's where I went to,' said the postman. 'I was intending to go on through Bantry and Glengarriffe but I didn't.' We cycled on in silence for a few moments but he didn't offer to explain his change of plan. 'Did you ever hear the story of Leap?' he asked at last.

'No,' said I. 'What story is that?'

'About the priest that was being hunted by the English, and he took a leap across the pass, and they say the print of his fingers is in the rock to this day?'

'Yes,' said I. 'I heard that.'

'And would you believe it?' the postman asked curiously.

'I imagine it's only an old legend,' I replied doubtfully. (I must have a trace of English blood in me somewhere. I knew that wasn't the proper answer or the one the postman was expecting.)

'But there's a poem about it,' he persisted.

'Is there?' I asked.

'There is,' said the postman. 'I'll say it for you.'

And while we pushed slowly up a long hill on the edge of the Galtees and Célimène lagged behind, he recited for me every word of a longish poem in the manner of Walter Scott. It was the sort of poem you still find on the magazine page of the local weekly accompanied by a pen-and-ink drawing of an ivy-covered castle.

'You have a good memory anyway,' said I, praising the only thing I could find to praise in it.

'Ah, I have that by heart since I was a child,' confessed the postman. 'You see, I took it for gospel, and I was always thinking that I'd like to see the mark of the priest's fingers for myself. So at last I got up on the old bike and went off there. But when I got to Leap the people only laughed at me. They thought I was a fool. It seems like yourself they have no great belief in it. . . . Good morning now,' he added politely as he sheered off up a by-road.

'Good morning,' I cried after him, and while I unpacked our kit by the lee-side of a church and Célimène went into a cottage for boiling water, I was weeping and laughing to myself at the postman's adventure. Célimène, I feel, thought I was a little hysterical. Even today I doubt if she really understands why I carried on like that. Perhaps it is because I am a little in the same line myself.

But that was not the end of the matter. Nature is not generally given to artistic composition, having quite enough business of her own to attend to, but when she does take it in hand, she shows remarkable talent. A couple of hours later we stopped again on the outskirts of Tipperary and laid out our midday meal in a field before a row of little cottages. It was my turn to look for the hot water. There wasn't any, but a motherly woman put the kettle on to boil while I sat in the kitchen with her. A few moments later the back door opened and a little man came in. He was small and wiry and spirited, with a slight moustache and blue eyes that danced with mischief.

'Welcome,' he said heartily with his hand outstretched. ''Tis only a humble place, but you're welcome to what's in it.'

I knew no Munster man would ever use a word like 'humble'. It is self-conscious and socialistic.

'You're not from these parts,' said I.

'No,' he replied, drawing himself up with a jerk of his shoulders. 'I'm a Belfast man. And what part do you come from?'

'Wicklow,' said I, more literally than truthfully.

'Man, dear,' he said with his eyes sparkling, 'I was only in Wicklow once, at a funeral, but I remember it well. It was only a wee woman we were burying, but the first round of drinks cost a pound.'

My heart warmed to him. He was a harness-maker by trade, and worked in a little space partitioned off by the window, and there was a seat against the partition inside. The window opened outward on to the street, and he had been there only a minute or two when someone stuck in his head.

'Come in, come in,' said the harness-maker impatiently, and the second man came in and planted himself on the bench behind the partition. I had the feeling that I had dropped into the parliament house of the neighbourhood, and that if I stayed long enough I should hear the troubles of the whole world discussed.

'You didn't come from Belfast here, did you?' I asked.

'No,' he said. 'I was working in Guinness's, but the blooming old doctor wouldn't pass me and they threw me out.'

'What was it?' I asked. 'Bad health?'

'No, bullets. I was in the last war.'

I knew there was something like that in it. Nobody could imagine that a man with a pair of eyes like that in his head had spent his whole life in Ireland.

'You ought to be thankful you're out of this one anyhow,'

I said, deliberately drawing him out, and perfectly well aware that, in the vivid phrase of the woman in the Ennistymon pub, that and drawing the razor across his throat were the two things ever farthest from his mind.

' Oh, indeed he ought,' agreed his wife, who was standing before the fire with her hands clasped on her apron, looking out the open door, and somehow I gathered that this was not the first time that particular remark had been made to him. ' God help us ! 'Tis awful ! All the poor people in London ! '

' And who the hell else started it ? ' snapped her husband, blazing out at her.

' Tut, tut, tut,' said his wife, and I felt I had butted in on a discussion which had been going on in one form or another for a considerable number of years.

' And who else, woman ? ' cried her husband. ' The London capitalists, with their money in German securities, that wouldn't let anyone say " Boo " to Hitler.'

' Tut, tut, tut,' she clucked again, wiping her hands in her apron, but she didn't say it by way of reproach or even in the way of a woman who was paying much attention, only out of a sense of duty to God and Ireland, taking it for granted that anything he said about ' capitalists ' must be unreasonable. ' Thanks be to God it didn't come here anyway.'

' Ah, De Valera is a great man,' I said, for sheer devilment, waving my red rag at him from behind her skirts, ' a great man to keep us out of it all this time.'

' He is so,' she agreed warmly, ' a great man.'

' We had enough of it ourselves,' I said firmly. ' We suffered our share.'

' Oh, God help us, we did,' she agreed.

' And what we need now is a bit of peace and quietness,' I added.

' Peace and quietness ? ' the harness-maker echoed in a tone of resignation, looking at the ceiling. ' Young man, will I tell you what's wrong with this country ? Nothing ever happens here, that's what's wrong with us. Nothing ever happened here since two thousand years before Christ.'

But he knew I was only drawing him out. He was probably glad to be drawn out. A man who has to live in a town like Tipperary is probably glad of anyone to explode on. I once lived with a man in a small country town, and in the evenings when he came in from work he always exploded on me. He had a manuscript case, and the first thing he did was to kick it about the room like a football. Then he took up a Greek play and read me a speech from it of which I didn't understand a solitary word. He asked me if I couldn't feel the sunlight in it ; but I couldn't, not very much. Then he said he was a child of the sun banished up in the bloody North Pole among fogs, ice-floes and Eskimos. Once I asked him whether there was anybody else in the town whom he could talk to as he talked to me. He said there was, a publican.

' And what do you say when you meet him ? '

' I say " —— ." (You will have no difficulty in supplying the missing word.)

' And what does he say ? '

' He says " —— ? " And then I say " ——," and he says " ——." And we go on till we've exhausted all the dirty words we know, and then we settle down and have a chat.'

And if I were to go back tomorrow and discover that the harness-maker was gone, I shouldn't be in the least surprised. As I say, Nature does not indulge much in artistic composition, but when she does she shows great talent, real talent.

## 14

BETWEEN the western wind and the small rain, the towns that are bad for a cup of tea and the ruins of churches and castles that no one cares for, the usual danger with Célimène and myself is misanthropy, but the sure hands of the wind, catching us by the shoulders and pushing us on, induced a sort of expansive mood of universal benevolence in which people plan new economic and political systems with a lordly indifference to circumstances. Cahir was clean and it had a fine castle guarding the bridge over the Suir (the one Essex captured), a millwheel, and a row of little houses by the weir with their sun-blinds out. In the railway station there were rambler roses up the lamp-posts and buckets of flowers on the platform. Célimène went into a shop to buy two oranges and they treated her as if it were an order for export. She said it reminded her of an English town, than which she knows no higher praise. (I don't say Cahir is always or even usually like that; it would probably be different when the wind was blowing from the other direction.)

The castle, being in private hands, was in excellent repair, and when we entered it by a wicket gate we found ourselves in a long garden with a woman cutting flowers and a dog yapping at her heels. The housekeeper told us that the ladies of the town had held a ' carnival ' there, and whether it was that or the reminiscence of some English market town, Célimène sniffed the breeze and tossed her mane.

' You could do a play here,' she said.

Now, as a general rule, I am old and cynical enough to be able to restrain her enthusiastic fits, but the wind had also in-duced a pleasant haze of enterprise in me, and instead of mocking I encouraged her. While she was setting up the stage and arranging the lighting I was toying with the idea of a historical tragedy. I had once seen Hauptmann's *Florian Geyer* in the hall of Heidelberg Castle and never forgotten it. I even had a subject to my hand from a genealogical tract dealing with the Butlers and Fitzgeralds, the two great Norman families who divided southern Ireland between them. The Butlers, being eighty miles nearer London, maintained their connection with England, but the Fitzgeralds allowed themselves to be absorbed by the Irish families about them, and one of the earliest, Earl Gerald, became famous as a love poet in Irish. He has become a minor Celtic divinity and lives under Lough Gur in Co. Limerick.

The story deals with a girl called Catherine Fitzgerald who got into trouble at home about a love affair with some cousin and stormed out in a temper, bringing her women and chaplain with her. The chaplain was in love with her — so I suspect was the old genealogist, because whenever he speaks of her he gives us what he thinks must have been her own words, and what is that in a story-teller but love ?

She took refuge with the Earl of Gowran at his castle. The Earl, like all the Butlers, had married an Englishwoman, Isabel by name, and had a son and daughter by her. One day, when he was ill in bed, Catherine and her women went to visit him. Some fashionable new dresses of the countess were lying about the room, and Catherine for sport put them on. The other women shrieked and gibed at her. ' Fie ! Fie ! ' called the Earl. ' What is all this about ? ' ' They are laughing at me,' replied Catherine, ' seeing me in English clothes. If it is English clothes that make Englishwomen so attractive I must be attractive now. You Irish earls imagine you'll never find a wife in Ireland good enough for you, but I fancy I'm a better Countess now than the hag you've got.'

Something about the little scene impressed the man, for soon after he made her his mistress — raped her, the genealogist would have us believe, and given the sort of woman he describes, that is psychologically credible. Isabel and her children cleared out and went to live in Waterford. The scandal reached the ears of Catherine's father. He charged Butler with it, and

Butler, unknown to his mistress, sent a message offering him satisfaction, and arranging a meeting on the bank of the Suir at a place called Aylenamearogue, near the Cistercian monastery of Inishlounaght outside Clonmel. They met at opposite sides of the river, and Butler invited Fitzgerald to cross. As the party reached the water Fitzgerald's horse stooped to drink, the bridle slipped over his ears between his feet, and he tripped and fell, throwing his master head foremost into the river. As he wore heavy armour he was drowned at once.

While the meeting was taking place unknown to her, Catherine was working out a plot of her own. She sent her chaplain down the river with a present of Zante wine for the Englishwoman in Waterford. Butler imported it direct through Youghal, and in case Isabel had any suspicions, the chaplain was given the Earl's signet ring to show. The wine was received and drunk by Isabel and her daughter. Young Richard came in later and asked for some too, but the chaplain boxed his ears and told him he was too young to begin drinking. As the chaplain crossed back over the ferry to the Kilkenny bank the bells in the city were tolling for the death of Isabel and her daughter. The wine had been poisoned.

Butler returned home, having warned his followers to say nothing to their mistress of her father's death. Catherine rushed out joyously to meet him. 'I have news for you,' she cried, 'if you'll pay.' 'I'll pay,' said Butler. 'The English countess and her daughter are dead.' Then a great sadness came over the Earl and he added, 'I have news for you too, if you'll pay,' and told her of her father's death. 'After that', adds the genealogist, with the air of Flaubert ending a story that threatens to become too dramatic on him, 'the Earl put her away and Fitzthomas had her.'

A grim little story: in Scotland the names would have been Douglas and Percy, and the incident would have become the subject of a Border ballad. In Ireland it just serves to lift the curtain on the relationship between the two great families which is so dreadfully over-simplified in the history books.

As we were leaving the gardener advised us not to miss a sight of Carrick Castle on our way down the Suir, and being still in the same state of enterprise, we resolved to spend the night there. In that pleasant haze with the wind still behind us, the distance seemed nothing. We drifted on towards Slievenamon, slumped over the valley till we saw the long green hill that glides down to the Suir at Clonmel and freewheeled gaily down the principal street, under the town gate, past George Borrow's old school, where he had the 'opportunity of making acquaintance with all the Protestant young gentlemen of the place, the handsome well-dressed young persons whom your honour sees in the church on Sundays, when your honour goes there in the morning with the rest of the Protestant military, for it is no Papist school, though there may be a Papist or two there'. The Tholsel, here for some reason called the Main Guard, closed the street in a dazzle of reflected light. All these eighteenth-century Tholsels and market-houses are adorable, but owing to the absence of public lavatories, almost every one has had its arcade bricked up. In Clonmel it had been turned into shops, which isn't quite so bad. The green of the hillside could be seen through every lane. As we dismounted Célimène shivered.

'What is it?' said I.

'Nothing,' she said. 'I had the feeling that that hillside was moving.'

The woman was prophetic. We had our supper on the river-bank beside a hump-backed bridge with a charming Georgian mall below it, and I began to feel the hillside moving too. First, the enterprise drained rapidly away. We took a room in a hotel, and walking up the main street passed three pairs of good-looking girls unattended. I reflected that it was probably one of those towns described by Géronte 'where all the young men are old men and all the old men are old whores'. We passed a group of women in shawls who jeered at us. We passed a boarded-up pub which in Ireland always signifies the beginning of the end. Then we came to George Borrow's school, and found that deserted too.

'Maybe you'd like to look round inside, sir?' said a man's voice behind us.

'Why?' I asked. 'Isn't there anyone in it?'

'Well, no, sir. There were people one time thinking of taking it for a school, but it seems the teachers' rooms had a bad aspect. Then the military were thinking of taking it over, but the officers that inspected it said there was no place in it for artillery.'

'That's bad,' said I.

'It is, sir. Will I show you round?'

'We'll see tomorrow,' said I, feeling I had enough to depress me. To get away from it we crossed the river and came down the further bank. It was pleasant there with Slievenamon and the white campanile of the Catholic church reflected in the water opposite the old boathouse. We re-entered the town by a foot-bridge and found ourselves in a complete suburb of eighteenth-century mills and warehouses, all in ruin. As we stood by a tall rusty gate, looking at a handsome old mill-house with the weeds growing like thatch on its parapet, the bats swooped down on us. We fled for comfort to the mall we had seen from the bridge at supper-time, but when we reached it we saw a glass porch patched with cardboard and windows gaunt against the night sky and heard the sound of rats pattering in the ruins. As we continued along the river-bank an Irish terrier padded silently before us with a big rat dangling from his jaws. Above the old bridge we came on a seat under the trees, and on the seat a Franciscan monk was smoking between two good-looking girls. When we stopped they both modestly lowered their eyes.

'Can we get back to the town if we continue along this bank?' I asked him.

'Oh, to be sure ye can,' he replied in an unctuous voice, flicking the ash off his cigarette. 'Ye can cross the fields any-where ye like.'

'I suppose there's no footpath?' said I.

' Ah, no one will mind ye crossing the fields,' he said smoothly, ' You know,' he added blandly, cocking his tonsured pate at us, ' we're a liberal sort of people down here.'

As a matter of fact, I had been thinking that, though ' liberal ' wasn't exactly the word I would have used. Something about Clonmel reminded me of Cork ; the same warm, dim, odorous, feckless, evasive southern quality, and the last drop of enterprise oozed away. When we got back to the main road we found ourselves passing the ruins of a huge barrack — the cavalry barrack where Borrow's father had been stationed with the rest of the Protestant military. At that we began to laugh, and we split our sides when two children followed us to the hotel, begging persistently and vociferously. The town cinema, being Gaelic-minded, called itself after Ossian, and it might have been quite appropriate if it had been showing ' The Walls of Balclootha '. Unfortunately, the picture of the week was ' Naughty but Nice '.

' Oh, yes,' said the hotel boots in a melancholy voice, ' Clonmel used to be a very important place at one time.'

' What time was that ? ' I asked, as sweetly as I could.

' Well, it was before my time,' replied the boots with great candour. ' Maybe a hundred years ago or so.'

' Or more,' said I.

' Or more,' agreed the boots.

' Two thousand years before Christ,' I thought, echoing the harness-maker.

Next morning as the bells were ringing for Mass we loaded up the bikes and I studied the map.

' What about the grammar school ? ' said Célimène, who likes to see whatever there is to see.

' To hell with the grammar school,' said I.

' And the parish church is supposed to contain traces of twelfth-century work,' she persisted, looking at the guide-book.

' It can keep them,' said I, and away we went for Carrick.

## 15

THE trip down the Suir in the morning light was something you wouldn't be likely to forget. The river, growing broader and stronger, began to throw up hills on either side, and the hills were dotted with grey keeps of the Butlers. Carrick itself turned out to be a snug little town well dug in under the Waterford mountains with a high hilly street of purple sandstone climbing their sides, and a charming little market-house. Though we never suspected it, there was a pig-buyer in Carrick that morning who paid particular attention to us. That fact will emerge in due course, but as a dramatist I like to prepare for my entrances.

The castle which the gardener in Cahir had recommended was down a little cul-de-sac by the river, and when we reached the main gate there was a notice that said ' Visitors are Requested Not to Beat Carpets in the Vicinity of the Castle '. We hadn't brought any carpets, but the notice gave us the idea that the people in the castle were not ones you could treat lightly. We went up the avenue more or less on tiptoe, and stood at the far side of a bedraggled stretch of lawn from the castle. It wasn't a castle but a fine Tudor manor-house.

Now Tudor manor-houses may be three a penny in England, but in Ireland they don't exist at all, and we stood there lost in admiration of the three gables, and the windows with their diamond panes, and the tall chimney-pots against the background of trees. Behind the manor-house was the battlemented, ivy-covered keep of the real castle. We didn't like to approach nearer for fear someone might suspect us of having carpets concealed. As I was taking a photograph a middle-aged woman came out from behind the house, shooing some hens before her. I went up and apologised for intruding.

' Maybe you'd like to have a look round inside ? ' she suggested.

I nearly said 'Would we hell!' but recollected my manners in time and said I hoped we wouldn't be disturbing the family.

'I'm the only one who lives here now,' she said.

I didn't fully understand the meaning of that till we went into the hallway and she asked us to mind ourselves on the stairs. In places they stopped and then went on again. It was plain then that she wasn't one of the family. Whoever they were, they didn't live here any more.

Upstairs she showed us into a splendid room that ran the length of the house with a deep window embrasure flooded with sunlight and what had once been a magnificent stucco ceiling with a panelled frieze containing portraits of Queen Elizabeth; but below the frieze the room had been stripped of its oak panelling; the ornamental fireplace had been removed; floor and ceiling above us had both caved in so that the laths were hanging down and the plaster had been heaped up against the walls. It was a nasty mess.

'Who owns this place?' asked Célimène, her eyes flashing with tears.

'The Marquis of Ormonde, ma'am. He couldn't afford to keep it up, so he carried away the wood and the fireplace to Kilkenny Castle.'

This was the fireplace we had seen in the library at Kilkenny.

'Queen 'Lisbeth,' added our guide with a smile, pointing to what remained of the frieze.

Then she opened the door of a smaller room which overlooked the river-bank. Every pane of glass in the beautiful window had been shattered and lay about the floor with the plaster.

'This is the room Anne Boleyn was born in,' she said.

'It looks like the room she was killed in,' said I.

'It is the school children who do that,' she replied apologetically. 'They pass along the river-bank on their way home from school.'

'They certainly are a credit to their education,' said I.

Célimène was just refraining from breaking down. Good

buildings like all thoroughbreds should be put quietly out of pain, and not left to drag out a miserable existence when their great days are done. But it was plain that our guide had long ago ceased to notice the dilapidation that went on about her. She was a good-natured, obliging woman. She showed us another room with a stone fireplace and a Latin inscription running about the frieze. 'Fireplace,' she said with a smile, pointing to the first, and 'Latin,' she added, pointing to the second. She reminded me rather of the way I speak French — a noun eked out with a smile.

She showed us into another small room. 'This is the room Anne Boleyn was born in,' she repeated, and I didn't trouble to ask her how Anne managed to get born in so many places at once, because anyway, Anne couldn't have been born there at all. But it did strike me as a queer sort of existence for a woman of her kind, living alone in that magnificent house which was falling to ruin under her eyes. This, I thought idly (not in the least with the conviction with which I had felt the same sort of thing outside Monaincha), would be the sort of house to see ghosts in. And as I wondered what sort of ghosts there would be, I suddenly recollected the story of Catherine Fitzgerald which I had been thinking of in the hall at Cahir Castle. I remembered that it was in the Butler castle of Carrick-on-Suir that she had taken refuge when she left home with her chaplain and maids — not indeed this house nor even the castle behind the house, for both were long after her time.

'You're not afraid to live here alone?' said I.

'Ah, wisha, no, sir, I'm not,' she replied with the same good-natured smile.

'And you don't see any ghosts?'

'Indeed I don't, sir. 'Tis the living I'd be afraid of.'

'You have a better nerve than I have,' said I.

'Ah, if you were brought up in a place like this, as I was, you wouldn't be frightened of it,' she said.

'Oh,' said I. 'You've always lived here, then?'

'Oh, no, sir, I haven't. I was out of it for a long time. Then my aunt that was the old caretaker got sick and I came back to mind her. I wasn't going to stop when I saw what 'twas like. When I was a girl it used to be grand.'

' It must have been lovely,' said Célimène, and we were both thinking that it must have been a grand place for a child to grow up in and explore, a marvellous place for fancy to develop.

' It was, ma'am, lovely,' she said simply. ' But then they took away the wood and the fireplace, and it all got neglected. I didn't think I could ever stop. And then — ah, well, I suppose you get used to things ! Ye'd like to see the old castle ? '

' We would,' said I.

' I won't go with ye,' she said, showing us a plank that led from an open landing across to the keep. ' I'm getting too old for climbing.' This part of the house must have been the chapel for there were remains of stucco angels high up in the wall. We mounted the stair to the tower which overlooked the tall Tudor chimney-pots, and gave us a pleasant view up the river of the little purple town ensconced under the Waterford mountains. It was up there that I told Célimène the story that had come back into my mind the previous day in Cahir, and it took on a new reality as we leaned over the battlements and could look up the river towards Clonmel the way Butler returned from his meeting with Catherine's father at Inishlounaght, and down the river towards Waterford from which the pathetic and sinister priest rode back after the murder of Isabel and her daughter.

Then somewhere deep down in my memory I recollected that there was some other connection with Cahir Castle. What was it ? I couldn't remember, and it wasn't until I got back home that I was able to look up what the old genealogist said about it. ' It was this daughter of the Earl of Desmond ', he wrote, ' who bore James the Englishman to the Earl of Ormond, and James the Englishman's race are the Butlers of Cahir-on-Suir.' Maybe it isn't Carrick but Cahir that is haunted by her tempestuous little ghost. A troublesome, dissatisfied ghost she must be if she ever appears as Célimène and I had been planning to show her, in the hall of the old castle, because surely no love story in the world has a more melancholy end than hers. 'After that the Earl put her away and Fitzthomas had her.'

We remained there for a long time looking across the little town to the hills, as she and her lover may have done. When we went down again the caretaker was waiting for us in the hall to show us some pictures that nobody had thought worth taking away. One was a damned ugly crucifixion which rather looked as though one of the Kilkenny masons of the sixteenth century had turned his hand to painting. 'Canvas,' she said, pointing to it with a smile. The others were two faded portraits on glass in the hall. 'Glass,' she added, pointing them out to us.

In that desolation there was something appropriate in the woman who seemed to be speaking in a foreign tongue. It added another dimension — of remoteness.

## 16

ACTUALLY, I dodged Cork as long and as hard as I could. We cycled up the coast from Waterford to Youghal, and when we got to Youghal, instead of continuing on our way to Berkeley's old church at Cloyne, we doubled off up the Blackwater to Lismore. Partly, of course, it was because Lismore was the headquarters of the twelfth-century reformers, and Cormac MacCarthy had given it two chapels; partly because Myler MacGrath had a family tomb there.

All that remains of Cormac's two chapels are a couple of carved stones built into the west wall of the cathedral, one a particularly fine figure of a Romanesque bishop. Myler's tomb had been kicked to the back of the nave by way of dissociating him from the church. It was one of his numerous dioceses, and he gave the castle to Raleigh by way of a present. The church is interesting as an example of fifteenth-century work rebuilt in the seventeenth century, and the only one I know which could by any stretch of the imagination be described as Perpendicular. Myler's successors in the castle now form the bulk of its diminished congregation — thirty-two when we were there. It is a pity, for it is a nice church, and (always excepting the monstrous ugliness of the Catholic cathedral) Lismore is as charming a town as there is in the south, full of lovely houses. The houses were the very things the beautiful girl in the bar objected to.

' Ach, it's a dead-and-alive old hole,' she said.

' What's wrong with it ? ' I asked.

' It's the houses,' said the girl with a twinkle. ' This is the only town in Munster where you can get houses cheap, and whenever a bank clerk gets married he's sent here.'

' Oh ! ' said I. ' But haven't you any other amusement ? '

' Not very much.'

' Haven't you even a dramatic society ? '

' We had, but it split.'   (Dramatic societies in country towns always do.)

' Or a library ? '

' That's run by a whole lot of old women, and whenever a decent book arrives they make away with it.'

' But haven't you *anything* to do ? '

' Ah, well,' she said hopefully, ' there's a twopenny library starting down the street, and then we'll probably get something to read.'

But when I proposed cycling from this to Killarney Célimène began to suspect she was being cheated of something, and I had to explain to her as well as I could that a writer who goes back to his native place is rather in the position of Heine's monkey chewing his tail.  Objectively he is eating, subjectively he is being eaten.

And yet, Cork is a charming town.   From our hotel window we looked down on the Regency bows and weather-slating of Patrick Street.   As the river flows everywhere beneath the street the Georgian basements are all on street level, so that front doors have a startling tendency to emerge half-way up the house in the manner of round towers, so high in fact that the steps which lead to them have to be built sideways along the front of the house.   Beyond and above the street, flat like a piece of theatrical scenery, was the hill above the river ;  the limestone portico of St. Mary's on the bank, the campanile of the presbytery above it, and between it and the Catholic cathedral, the adorable little tower of Shandon, two sides sandstone, two sides limestone, that peculiar blend which gives Cork its distinctive sombre colouring, particularly after rain.

Shandon, with its little turrets all boxed neatly into one another, always makes me a bit homesick for the Strand.   The only real trouble with Irish architecture is that its great period came half a century too late.  Its public buildings are too Roman, too declamatory.  It is an object lesson to stand for a quarter of an hour in College Green, taking a look now and again at the stolid grey screen of Trinity College and then resting your eyes on the curved complex front of Parliament House with its mysterious shadows or, disobeying the guide-book which sternly directs you to admire the Custom House and Four Courts, to wander into the Upper Castle Yard ('architecturally undistinguished', says my guide), which despite the blocking-up of its arcade and the addition of a hideous nineteenth-century porch, is still, with its red and cream uniform, as lovely and poetic as any little German court. St. Werburgh's, the Upper Castle Yard, Parliament House and Shandon, the tall doors with the broken pediment, you can number on the fingers of one hand the public buildings in Ireland that have this touch of Restoration fantasy —

> Oranges and lemons, say the bells of St. Clement's—

or

> Shandon Steeple stands up straight,
> Coppinger's Lane is undernate.

We cycled out to Kinsale, and the rain came in from the sea, thick and penetrating, and we shivered as we rounded the head of the bay at Belgooly. We ate our lunch in the fishermen's shelter out of the rain. Opposite us was Scilly with its white fishermen's cottages on a smooth green hill, and behind us the weather-slated, bow-fronted houses clung to the face of the cliff wherever they could secure a foothold, leaving no room for anything but rocky lanes that wound in and out between them. Having no street, the town was all odd unexpected corners with a square the size of a boxing ring, and room for very little but a tiny market-house with slated turret and gables and an *open* arcade. The parish church, with its ivy-clad tower splayed to the thrust of the hill, was all tapered, wall and tower in the Irish manner, but except for little idiomatic touches like that and the nave arcade, it might have been any parish church in any little English fishing village. Adjusting our capes as we came out, we saw a funeral go by, the coffin shouldered in the traditional way by four men, all the same name as the corpse, and the women hobbling along behind in their traditional hood cloaks. It was easy to see that Gaelic Ireland was seeping back.

But the thing I shall remember longest was the Big House. We cycled out to it along the river on a showery morning, trusting to luck to secure us admittance. Churches are one thing, but private houses are another, and depend heart-breakingly on the whims of their owners. When we got to the village we enquired the way and were told it.

'Do you think we'd be allowed to see the house?' asked Géronte, and for the first time I realised that that placid man was in a state of anxiety worse than my own.

'Ah, I'm sure you will,' said the labourer we asked.

'What did you say the name was?' asked Géronte, though the man hadn't said anything at all.

'A Mrs. ——,' replied the villager. 'She's only in it a month.'

'But she's a decent sort?' asked Géronte.

'Ah, she is,' said the labourer, and then he grinned at Géronte and me. 'Anyway, it's up to yeerselves to get under her skin.'

I admit the thing doesn't sound well, but when a man wants to see something in the way of architecture, it is surprising to what depths he will descend. For some time I had been noticing a certain decline in my own character, but I was astonished to see the same thing in Géronte. We opened the gate and went up the avenue, opened another gate, still without a glimpse of the house, and suddenly found ourselves before an adorable little Queen Anne house, slated on the weather side in the usual Cork manner. There was another bow-fronted house built on to it. The hall door was open, with a magnificent knocker shaped like a lyre. Inside was a dilapidated but beautiful semi-circular hallway with a frieze of rams' heads and two narrow doors with tiny fanlights to either side. A dog came out and began to jump on me with muddy paws but I did not protest. Then he transferred his attention to Géronte who positively hugged him. The man's character was revealing staggering depths of duplicity.

And then, as if startled by the light sound of the delicate

little knocker in the empty hall, one of these awful 'I have been here before' feelings overcame me, and with a sinking at the pit of my stomach I looked round at Célimène, Géronte, the dog and the old farmyard, searching for something about the scene which would not be familiar; but everything was bathed in that unnatural light in which we seem to be out of ourselves, watching ourselves perform actions which we know have already been performed, the mind aloof, the body an automaton. I know that it is generally supposed to mean that we have foreseen the event in a dream, and Dunne has ingeniously demonstrated that the precognition is the act of an immortal Observer in a region where the events of Time are simultaneous. But as the moment faded, and the composition of people and landscape became unfamiliar again, I realised that the immortal Observer in me had unaccountably omitted to observe the really important thing, and that I still didn't know whether or not I had got into the house.

As a matter of fact, I had, but apparently only just. The occupant at that time — I mean the present occupant, but these peculiar events produce a certain confusion of tenses — had only been in possession a month; we were the first visitors who had called to see it; the house was untidy, and anyway there was nothing to see but the dining-room. (That was a fib, but anyone who has only been a month in a big farm-house would almost certainly tell the same story.)

'But it's only the dining-room we want to see,' we said pleadingly.

'Oh, well,' she said, 'I suppose since you've come so far,' and she opened the door in the middle of the semicircular hallway, and showed us into one of the loveliest small rooms in Ireland. It had been decorated by the two Francini brothers for the English Bishop of Cork in the first half of the eighteenth century. Their known work is small; Carton and Castletown outside Dublin, and two town houses in Stephen's Green. The ceiling was a plaster copy of a Poussin picture, and the walls were panelled with scenes, of which we with small Latin and less

Greek identified only Aeneas bringing Anchises out of Troy. It was all whitewashed, scarcely the way the Francini left it, but the tapestry in the plaster frames between the panels was still intact. A lovely room, though one panel had recently been injured by rain.

'You can see what a bad state we found the roof in,' said Mrs. ——, pointing it out to us. 'While the place belonged to the Brown estate there was always a clause that compelled the tenants to keep this room in repair.'

'Whom does it belong to now?' we asked.

'The Land Commission,' she said. 'They dropped the clause out of the lease. My husband was at me when we bought it to knock down the house and build a decent modern one.'

'That would be a pity,' we said, aghast, realising for the first time how easily a masterpiece may disappear and no one the wiser.

'That's how I felt about it,' she said. 'Of course, it is a drain. You could throw a thousand pounds into a place like this and never notice the difference. On the other hand, if you did get it right you'd have something good to show for your money.'

She took us round to show us the front of the house, and on the way we passed the bow where the workmen had dumped a cartload of rubbish from the channel between the two roofs. Géronte was quick to notice the beautiful fireplace while Célimène spotted the carved shutters. The lady of the house blushed.

'You could have seen that,' she said, meaning that we couldn't, and we took shelter from a heavy shower under a great tree beside the bow. 'Of course, I haven't had much time, with seventy-five acres, and the trouble of getting men to work. You'd want to go with a pony and trap to fetch them. The previous tenant wasn't able to do much, living here alone.'

'An old woman?'

'Not so old. It seems she was always in dread of this tree falling on her. She lived in the one room there with the bow window. I don't suppose even if it did fall it would do much harm. Those old walls would stand more than that.'

'And what happened her?' I asked.

'Well, a funny thing, it must have been fright. There was a big storm a little while ago. It broke one big bough off that tree in the middle of the field. When the milkman called next morning he got no reply, so he brought a ladder and looked in her bedroom window. She wasn't in the bed, but just as he was coming down again he saw her by the window. It seems she must have heard the branch coming down, and thought it was this one.'

The rain cleared, the sun came out with sudden brilliance, and we wanted to go further while it lasted.

'I was offered £180 for the fireplace,' she added with growing confidence, 'and my own price for the knocker. It seems 'tis valuable.'

'It looks it,' said Géronte.

'I told the auctioneer I didn't buy the place to scatter it,' she said with sudden spirit. I think in a way she wasn't al-together sorry that we had called. She must have had fits of wondering whether after all her practical husband wasn't right. But women are all fetish worshippers, and it matters little to them whether the fetish is of their own tribe or, like that house of Bishop Brown's, something the tide has washed to their feet. So long as it is an image of something in their hearts they will sacrifice life and happiness to it. But it is a hard service that the fetish exacts, and Géronte knew it, and wondered if her courage would last. Women, sleeping in one room of some great house in its woods, going to bed hungry rather than part with granddad's cracked portrait, women lost to the world like mystics in the contemplation of God, know how hard that service can be.

## 17

IN my boyhood there were never more than two real roads out of Cork. One was the one we had taken, through Midleton to Youghal, a pleasant green country full of big houses. It too has its ruined castles, but you feel they have done their job and can take their rest. In Carrigtwohill we went to have a look at the castle, which is very much like most castles of its date in Ireland, with four angle towers, and the big living-rooms in the central keep. There was a whitewashed farm-house at the foot, and again I got back an old regret that I hadn't been brought up in a farm-house like that, with a great cliff of a ruined castle to retire to when I wanted to think. I used to retire to a hole in the face of a big quarry, but that is not the same thing as winding stairs and little arched rooms with lancet slits that take in a sunlit picture of a bridge. There must be something wrong about people who can't grow excited about castles.

This was a good ruin. From the top storey we could look down through a ruined floor at the remains of a big arched window in the hall, and framed in its cool grey a picture of hens scratching on a heap of dung in brilliant sunlight. Beside it was another ruin, which Géronte suddenly identified as the remains of a small Jacobean manor-house. I got through the wire and unlocked the door, but as I went in a big bull stood up and stared at me. We went on to Midleton, a pleasant town with a pleasant market-house, and had our tea above a little shop in the main street. It was a good cup of tea. The castle could afford to be pensioned off. It had completed its work of civilisation.

But the castles on the other road have a frustrated air. This and not the tamed road to the east it was that used to excite us in our boyhood. First, it passed a tapering tower standing on the river-bank among meadows, then wound uphill through the woods at Inishcarra, and after that the river began to drop away, and the road was quarried out of a wall of rock. A few miles out we caught our first glimpse of the West Cork mountains : Shehy, Douce and Doochil, very blue and far away. We saw them again where the country rose in a pine-clad hillside, and then the road went on again between beeches whose shadows flowed over us in waves, and through their blue colonnade we caught glimpses of the river beneath.

We made our first halt at Macroom. The old town had a nice market-place with a charming market-house and a burned-out castle ('we burned it') dominating the Ballyvourney road. There was an interesting door in the castle and a good pub in the main street, and we carried on along a tree-shadowed by-road and up the long hill of Rossmore while Géronte continued to sing the praises of the sweet pint he had drunk in Macroom. The country mounted on either side of us in bleak grey hills ; gradually it came closer to the road, all choppy like a sea, threatening it here and there in bumpy, grassy hillocks, till all at once, as we reached the top of the hill and began our free-wheel down into Inchigeela, it rose and hurled itself on us, snapping at us with red sandstone teeth between purple lips of heather. All about us the hillsides, russet with withered furze, were stretched till the skin of soil cracked on their stony quarters, and in the deep hollows were patches of wet, jade-green grass or little triangular fields of golden corn, where the sunlight went to earth.

It moved me so much that in Inchigeela, the first Irish-speaking village we came to, I asked for two whiskeys in the native tongue. I was considerably sobered when the girl brought us two glasses of stout instead. Of course, I could have pointed out that *ishge baha* is not the Irish for stout, but it might have hurt her feelings, and anyway it served me right. But Géronte was furious. I have never seen him so furious except on one occasion when a Catholic hotel refused to give him bacon and eggs on Friday. All the bigotry of his Cromwellian ancestors rose up in him. 'If you speak that bloody language again,' he said savagely, 'I'll go home.' We stood in the porch of the hotel, watching a bearded, begging friar go from door to door with a gladstone bag, and a horse and cart following at a respectful distance.

Ballingeary was a hamlet of fir and sycamore with a brown stone church facing the whitewashed school-house, and little rows of astonished farm-houses whose top windows had been continued into the roof in dormers. They looked as if they had never got over the shock. In the pleasant, windy mountain church there were two handsome Renaissance altars, one with red and one with blue curtains, but altars and curtains were only painted on the whitewashed walls.

At this point I felt that even Christianity was wearing thin. As we left the little village my heart began to leap again as it leapt when I was a boy, for the wild rush of the river down the rocks, the whitewashed farm-houses and little steep fields, with their gipsy brightness among the desolation. Beside a cottage that stood sideways to the little mountain road was an old woman with a man's hat plastered down over her white locks. She had a face like the Muse of Tragedy, an unforgettable face.

'Where's the Tailor from you, Anstey?'

'He's up there on the brow of the hill with a couple of childher.'

And there, by the road, with his withered leg stretched out, his round, yellow, baby face, his piercing little eyes, was the Tailor, teaching Irish to a couple of city childher. He was a little leprechaun of a man, a rural Dr. Johnson. A couple of years ago, a young visitor from England wrote down some of his stories and sayings, and then the old man's troubles really began. The book was banned by the Irish Government as 'indecent', Government spokesmen described him as 'a dirty old man', and a gang of priests made him burn the book at his own hearth.

We left him to look for a meal. The black mountain, all vertical lines, swooped down to the lake, where a few fields of unearthly pallor, and all in horizontal lines, were reflected in the still dark water. In the middle of the lake was an island with a modern chapel and a holy well. I remembered that two days before Michael Collins was killed a woman of the neighbourhood went to the well to pray for his death. She said it bubbled up to her. I could almost believe that. It is remarkable what you can believe in that valley. After supper we went back to the Tailor's. There was no row of neighbours there as there used to be, sitting along the settle behind his back, their hats over their eyes and their sticks clutched between their legs, but he went on with his story-telling and moralising. There never was a better story-teller or a more incurable philosopher. And that was the place, of a winter's night, to listen to stories about the fairies.

I remembered one night in particular when for the first time I seemed to understand the mingled attraction and repulsion of the place. We were talking of old-time priests, and another old man from up the hills described how one priest, a man with a wooden leg, used to chase the boys and young men who sat on the chapel wall after Mass had begun. I felt curious when I heard of the wooden leg.

'How did he come to lose the leg?' I asked.

'Ah, in a queer sort of way,' said the Tailor, and I knew I had put my foot in it. It was easy to see how. There was a priest in the party.

'Tell him,' urged the other old man, 'tell him, can't you?'

''Tis a queer story.'

'Even so! 'Twasn't you made it up.'

'It wasn't,' said the Tailor with that sudden smoothing of the round baby face that came to him in graver moments. 'You see,' he said, with his head bent forward, 'there was a man living there at the time called Con na bPucai — Con of the Fairies.'

'Why was he called that?' I asked.

'Because he was their Living Man,' said the Tailor.

'Their what?' said I.

'The fairies,' said the other old man eagerly, 'can do nothing without a Living Man. It is through him they act. They would call for him after dark, whatever it was they wanted to do.'

'Go on,' said I.

'And the priest was mad with him,' said the Tailor, taking up the story again. 'He was always giving out against him from the altar. He said it was superstition. One day he went up to the house to Con. "'Tis you," he said, "that's putting all this nonsense into the people's heads." And Con said, "Whose fault is it?"'

'He did, he did,' said the other man, nodding.

'"Who was it left four people die on the mountain without the sacraments?"'

'He did, that's true.'

'Because,' explained the Tailor, raising his hat reverently, 'the fairies are the souls of poor people that die without the priest. Very well,' he went on, slapping his knee. 'Soon after that the priest had a breaking-out on his knee. He went to the doctor, but the doctor could do nothing with it. He went then to the hospital in Cork, but they could do nothing with it. So he began to think it was Con that put the curse on him.'

I started. There it was, the whitewashed wall behind the painted Renaissance altar. It was easy enough to imagine that old country-bred priest, nursing his festering knee, and looking out at the rain falling in that desolate mountain country, while bit by bit whatever little education he had got at the seminary dropped away from him, and left him with nothing but the marvels and terrors that had been instilled into him from childhood. After all, wasn't it MacEvilly, the Archbishop of Tuam, who wouldn't allow the parish priest of Ballintubber to continue roofing the abbey church for fear of the fairies?

'So one day he got into the trap and went up to Con's.

'"This and that," he said, "this is your doing."

'"It is not, then," said Con.

'"Whose doing is it so?" asked the priest.

'"I'll tell you whose doing it is," said Con. "You were shot with a bow and arrow through the window of your own bedroom, and look now when you go back, and you'll see the little hole. And it was the Queen of the Fairies herself that shot you."

' " And how will I cure it ? " asked the priest.

' " You will never cure it," said Con. " That is the Queen's wound, and you might as well tell the doctors to take that leg off you, for 'twill never heal."

' And it didn't,' said the other old man.

' It did not,' said the Tailor regretfully, and I looked at them. I saw the glance of triumph in both their eyes. The young priest saw it too. He saw that in their eyes his religion was only a thing of yesterday. The moment passed.

' And tell me, Tailor,' said the priest, ' how is it the fairies are never seen now ? '

' I dare say it is the motor cars, father,' said the Tailor. ' Since the cars came there are few that die like that, thanks be to God.'

When Célimène, Géronte and I got up to go we found ourselves barricaded into the little cottage. A stump of a tree had been wedged against the door outside ; the persecution was still going strong. The old woman grew white with distress, but the Tailor comforted her. ' Whisht, whisht ! ' he said, with his brow growing smooth. ' At our age there is little the world can do to us.' Going back over the hill I could feel like an actual physical presence the sense of evil in the valley.

I stayed awake listening to the roaring of streams in the rain. In the middle of the night Célimène, fast asleep, crossed the bedroom and got into my bed. ' Don't be afraid,' she said through her dream. ' I'll protect you.' I didn't wake her, but I decided the Tailor was probably right. Motor cars have done a lot of good. Thanks be to God for motor cars !

# ❦ 18 ❦

KILLARNEY is a good business town. We had barely set foot in it when we were surrounded by four hotel porters who threatened to tear us asunder, and probably would have done so but that they quarrelled with one another first.

'Never mind him, ma'am. Their ould hotel is full.'

'Whose hotel is full?'

'They have a hundred of an excursion party from Cook's.'

'We have plenty of accommodation.'

We got away in the tumult, but one was too smart for us. He seized a bicycle from a passer-by — I suspect he knocked him down — and followed us. Having dodged him through the town, we were run to earth in a cul-de-sac.

'For Christ's sake don't persecute us!' I snarled.

'Oh, I'm sorry if I'm persecuting ye,' he said with a flush, and turned away.

He obviously thought he was doing us a good turn. In the shop where we went to buy our groceries for the road they told us that there had been a serious accident in which some soldiers were killed.

'Oh, how very sad!' said Célimène.

'Yes,' said the woman behind the counter. 'They brought in a lot of business.'

But in spite of the 'business' which makes it so wealthy, the few little vestiges of civilised life it contains are still in ruins. Culturally, it floats on a high tide of gab. The boatman who rowed us to the island knew nothing of the churches on it but tried to entertain us with O'Donoghue's Library and O'Donoghue's this and O'Donoghue's that. It is no trouble to them. Kerry men talk from the age of three months, and are conditioned to believe that language was invented to conceal thought. 'Father ——', we read in a local paper, 'is staying with his friend Father —— at the house of the latter's father. The advent of our young priests makes the sun to shine brighter and the wind blow sweeter from our lovely old hills.' And where was it I read that 'Mr. P. D——, N.T., then appeared and in a dulcet voice, sweetly reminiscent of Cordelia, announced that this would be the last whist drive of the season'. You cannot mistake the mellifluous idiocy of the true Kerry style.

There isn't very much to see there but the tremendous view from Aghadoe and the little Romanesque doorway, the main interest of which is that its peculiar capitals enable you to trace the mason who did it from Holy Island in Lough Derg, through Clonkeen in Co. Limerick. What happened him after he had designed the door in Aghadoe we cannot say. No doubt the hotel porters got him.

We went on to Tralee, another good business town, and a very pleasant one. We went to buy some butter in a dairy, and discovered that there were four of them, and that the customers bought their cream by the pint. We watched them buy it and saw the cream being ladled out of a churn. Sunday is the great day for cream ; on that day one dairy alone sells nine gallons. I was also informed, on the best authority, that the angels on local sepulchral monuments all wear buttoned boots.

The best thing in the neighbourhood of Tralee is the old cathedral centre of Ardfert seven or eight miles out, but this has been badly knocked about. It contains the remains of an admirable cathedral church and abbey in the Early English style, and a Romanesque chapel which must have been a beauty but is now savaged beyond restoration. The Gothic cathedral, beginning at the east end with a fine triplet of lancets, was apparently intended to take in the west front of the older, Romanesque cathedral, but missed its aim and came out with the remains of only three and a half arches on its buffers. These are of great interest, because they show that it must have been a front designed rather like that of Roscrea, and probably like Roscrea, deriving from Cormac's Chapel.

When we got back to Tralee there was the hell of a westerly

wind blowing; every time we tried to get up on our bicycles we were blown off them again, so we finally decided to take the bus as far as Dingle. It was race day and the bus was crowded. Just before it left an old gaol companion of mine got on. He was going to the races too, and it depended only on the company he struck up with, whether he came back that night or the next. And it wasn't that he wasn't fond of his wife, for he nearly fell off the bus waving to her as we passed his house. When I introduced him to Célimène he clutched her hand and absentmindedly held on to it for a matter of three miles. As it was the first time she had met a real Kerry man, she thought she'd better let him.

'Will the English win, do you think?' he asked. (We were talking of the war.)

'I sincerely hope so,' said I.

'You like them?' he added, screwing up his eyes at me.

'I do,' said I.

'Ah, they're nice,' he agreed with a flicker of a smile — we were both by way of being very anti-English in our youth. 'They are, mind you, very nice and very simple.' Curious, those were the very words used by the publican's wife in Rathdowney. Can it possibly be that Irish people think they are subtle? 'But a bit literal-minded, wouldn't you say?' he asked with a cock of the head. 'What? Oh, very literal-minded!'

'Now, I'll give you an example,' he went on, leaning over the back of the seat towards us. 'Just before the war I took my holidays in England, and I stayed in an inn with a couple of fellows I met while I was there — English chaps. Now, close to the inn there was a pond, and in the pond there was a pike; a hardy old brute of a pike that no one could ever catch. One of the English lads said *he'd* catch him. Well, I was interested, of course; naturally, for I'm a bit of a fisherman myself. So what did he do? He caught a bream, used the bream for a bait, and, begor, he caught the pike.

'Well, I was excited. Back with me to the inn, and I told the other fellows about it. Next morning one of them challenged me. "O'C——," says he, "didn't you say you caught that pike ? " " No," says I, " certainly I didn't. What makes you think that ? " " That's strange," says he. " I could have sworn you said you caught it."

' Now, that very evening, when the two of us were having a drink together, he turned on me again. " O'C——," he said flatly, " you *did* say you caught that pike." I began to rack my brains to know what I did say — by that time, of course, I hadn't the foggiest recollection, but it struck me that in my excitement I might have said " Well, boys, we caught the old pike "— just as we'd say it at home, you know, and it wouldn't mean anything only that the pike was caught. The pike was caught — that's all it would mean. But even that didn't satisfy him. The day he was going away, I went to the station to see him off. He was leaning out of the carriage window, shaking hands with me, and we were promising to write to one another, just as the train moved off. And then he shouted back at me, " Still, O'C——, you shouldn't have said you caught that pike."

' Now, what can you do with people like that ?

' Very funny people,' my friend continued thoughtfully. ' The same man was drinking with me one night in the bar, and he asked me if England was invaded would we come and fight for them ?

' " Oh, of course," said I. " To be sure we would."

' Man alive, that pleased him a lot ! I was the best in the world.

' " But now," says I, " tell me, supposing we're invaded, will ye do as much for us ? "

' " Oh," he said, " of course we shall have to do whatever our Government tells us."

' An extraordinary race ! '

A literal-minded man would get lost in West Kerry. Even I, the first time I came cycling in that direction, found my head spinning. I arrived at Dunquin after cycling round the coast from Cork, and, without knowing a sinner, I had walked up and down the road, looking for a pub. An old man sighted me from far up the mountain and bore down on me. At the same time three or four young men began to arrive from another direction. When I asked where I could find a pub, the old man enquired, ' What do you want a pub for ? '

Before I knew where I was I was in the middle of a furious argument on the evils of drink. I don't remember what the old man said against it, because there was another argument later about marriage and he contradicted himself flat, but I distinctly recollect what he would probably have called his ' peroration '.

' If you were a man that had a pound,' it began, ' and were to go into the town of Dingle, you could walk into a shop and buy one pig's head, or two pigs' heads or even three pigs' heads, and when you came home, you'd have fine feeding for your children and your wife would make love to you. But if you were a man that took a drink, every bummer in the town of Dingle would be round you for what he could get out of you, till your money was gone, and then "Hike to hell out of this, my man ! " and two policemen holding you behind.'

We started out from Dingle against the same fierce west wind which contested every inch of the road with us, and a spattering rain that chased us frequently to the uneasy shelter of a bush, but by the time we reached the brow of the hill, the wind had rent the awning of cloud, and little coloured rags of light fluttered through. We climbed a wall, battered by the wind. The view was magnificent. The sea was far away below ; at the mouth of the bay were Sybil Head and the Three Sisters, with the snout of Teeracht, black and vicious like something out of an El Greco background, showing round a headland to our left. Down the grey elephant pelt of the hills behind streamed the long lines of the fences, caught in the rush of the land as in a waterfall, wriggling and twisting and jumping in sudden cascades that dragged the little fields awry like faces drawn in pain, into cubes and triangles, each with its own pale, bright, almost hectic colour.

Brightest of all were the little chessboards of the cornfields where the stooks stood up in rows like golden chessmen. The whitewashed houses, poker-faced like the figures of playing cards, were caught up in the rush too, and stood not in the usual way of seaside houses, looking all in one direction like a crowd at the races, but staring stiffly in every direction out of the wind as if they had been halted in some fantastic drill. By the edge of the bay, where fields and fences grew bluer and paler, was a black spit of rock with a fountain of foam above it, and beyond it, the golden strand, with its silver waves foamed into phosphorescent mist, was filling the hollow of the hills with its distant booming. Above them the great low, ragged rain-clouds trundled eastward out of the Atlantic, searching the fields with the misty rays of their sun-lantern as if for something they had lost.

This was the Munster Thebaid where the old monks, inspired by the stories of the desert fathers, flocked in thousands, putting off humanity and building themselves little beehive huts and Eskimo oratories fitter for seagulls than men. The remains of these are scattered everywhere about the stony hills, and in the middle of them the little twelfth-century church, its front bleached snow-white by the terrible winds, its high gable soaring to the heart-shaped finial which in Irish churches took the place of a cross, seemed a strange lost outpost of European civilisation. The carved doorway had a tympanum — plain but still an unusual feature in an Irish church ; the north wall was panelled in half-columns which formed a frame for the windows, and there was a handsome little chancel arch much in the style of Cormac's Chapel. This is Cormac's country, and the church may even be another of his attempts to provide Ireland with a contemporary culture — poor man !

The wind was terrific, so we tried to boil our kettle in the chancel. We were interrupted by a stuttering child who suddenly appeared and joined his hands through a stone with a hole in it. ' B-b-b-bargain,' he stammered. We gave him sixpence for that. He went away and returned with a tall young man who talked to us for close upon an hour with unremitting zeal and mellifluousness. He seemed to be unusually interested in architecture. And then a dramatic thing happened. A tall, gaunt, Spanish-looking man stood under the tympanum of the little church and glowered in at us. The flow of mellifluousness dried up. The young man grew pale.

'A dangerous man,' he whispered to me.

The dramatic silence was unbroken for several minutes. Then the tall man began to mutter incoherently to himself in broken English. 'The mummers!' I heard him say. 'The mummers!' The stuttering boy made one wild dash and vanished. The tall young man drew himself up with great dignity and went quietly out past the newcomer, who drew aside and watched him go down the graveyard till he vanished from sight. I don't say I was frightened. I was petrified. It struck me that it was time Célimène and I also made ourselves scarce, but with some shadowy recollection of how one ought to behave, I paused nonchalantly in the doorway to point out to Célimène what I thought were the corbels of the wooden roof.

' 'Twasn't wood,' said the dangerous man in a laboured voice. 'It was shlates.'

'How do you know?' I asked in surprise.

'I pick them up,' he said. 'From graves. I am the caretaker.'

I sighed with relief. I understood at last the usurpation of 'the mummers', and the poor caretaker's indignation. He brought us to his little cottage to show us the second finial which he had dug up and put away for safety. I only wished all the Board of Works caretakers had half his intelligence, or indeed that the Board of Works — but there!

We cycled back to Tralee in an enormous, boisterous, windy sunset, when the little chessboards of the cornfields were slashed with long sloping shadows and the mountains seemed folding themselves for sleep. The silver shafts of the sun were like the arms of a giant mill-wheel, and, as it slowly revolved, the cascade of light wiped the hills clean of shadow and turned the telegraph posts wriggling up the hill into pillars of chalk. As we left the last brown stone village behind, the mountains seemed to grow larger and creep nearer till they crouched above us, their grey pelts glossy in the horizontal light. Darkness, swift and cold, fell before we reached the top. We shot downhill past Madman's Glen and along the shore of Tralee Bay as the moon rose, shouting joyously to one another. We might have been not a mere matter of miles but whole ages and continents away.

MY guide-book was enthusiastic on the subject of Mallow, and that gave us the itch to go back instead of proceeding up through North Kerry. 'Its bow-windows', said the book, 'give it an agreeable air of modishness', and though I had known Mallow and couldn't for the life of me remember anything modish about it, I assumed that this was because I saw it in days before I had learned to look at architecture. We paraded the town from end to end but failed to discover as much as one bow-window. (I think the guide-book meant 'bay-windows'.) Then we gave it up. On the other hand, going down a lane to the Protestant church, which proved inside and out to be an unmitigated horror, we found behind it the ruin of a really charming eighteenth-century church with a tower that looked considerably older. Why it was allowed to go to ruin we didn't enquire. Life is too short to discover the reason for all the ruins in Ireland.

From the moment we left Mallow we were into Geraldine country. In a way it is a reflection of the Butler country about Kilkenny; the same rich, flat, pastoral landscape which every Norman baron sought out; it is the landscape which Spenser described in *The Faerie Queen* but in a curious way its image is blurred — by the rain-clouds coming up the Shannon from the south or the blue hills of Kerry behind; most of all perhaps by the fact that it was beaten flat during the Desmond rebellions. It is mediaeval landscape which has been fused with prehistoric traditions, as the Norman blood of the Fitzgeralds was fused with the older blood of the little kingdoms. That gives it a poetic charm and a certain aimlessness. It can be magical at evening and at early morning; at noonday suffocating with its feeling of wealth and decay. A little river winding through flat country; an old bridge casually blown up in 'The Throubles';

the stump of a castle rooted like an old oak in some heap of rock by the river, blown up by Cromwell; the tapering tower of a ruined Franciscan monastery rising above a tall, slender chancel arch with an aisle and transept added to the nave in the clumsy style of the fifteenth century : that might be the picture of any Desmond township in Cork or Limerick.

Buttevant may serve as a type. When we asked the cattle dealer about a restaurant he put on a grave face and said, ' Buttevant is a bad town for a cup of tay.' They are all bad towns for a cup of tay. On the outskirts of the town in a rocky defile are the remains of a big Augustinian priory. These priories were really fortresses. That is why they could be built in open country. The ordinary Franciscan or Dominican convent was never until the fifteenth century built except in the shadow of an English castle. There isn't much of it there now, and what there is is used as the local byre and latrine. Under the tower there are some striking heads and two very fine gargoyles through which the bell-ropes passed.

In the main street is a second Franciscan church, built on a cliff overlooking the river, with a crypt beneath it. Not fifty yards away a perfectly aimless modern church has taken its place. At the end of the street is the ruin of a great military barrack burned during ' The Throubles '. (We burned it !)

I was stationed there at the time. Once, when we were attacking a parson's house in Co. Limerick which was occupied by the enemy, I was sent back to Buttevant barracks for ' the big gun '. The big gun, I found, was almost a legend. It had been begun before the Civil War, and for months the armourer who had made it had been piling up shells. By this time he had nine. He refused to be separated from his gun, so he took it in his arms and sat in the back of the car with it, nursing it as if it were a baby. Across the Limerick border we were met by another car in which was the officer in charge of the operation. He took the gun, and sent back the armourer to make more shells. The nine shells were fired at the parsonage but all of them landed wide. Then another officer came up to say that the enemy had escaped.

Charleville, by contrast, is a nice cheerful place though equally bad for a cup of tea. It had a charming little market-house (arcade bricked up, of course), a fine leather shop, and Binchy's lovely grocery shop of the eighteen-sixties or -seventies where they gave us beer and biscuits and cheese on a high stool in the counting-house. I enquired for a certain mechanic who was working in a garage in the town. I had a particular mournful interest in him because one Sunday morning twenty-odd years ago I motored in here from Buttevant barracks with dispatches for Kilmallock. The commandant of the local barrack, who was still in bed (it was nearly noon), told me the road to Kilmallock was clear of the enemy. It wasn't, as I discovered to my cost, for we had only gone a couple of miles out when we found the ditches lined by a party of men in indeterminate uniforms. Too late it dawned on me that it was Sunday morning, and that our front-line troops had gone off to Mass. 'Ate them,' said my driver, referring to the dispatches, but I never had much appetite for paper. As there was a high wind blowing I tore them up and scattered them. We were searched, and appropriately enough I had in my pocket a copy of *The Idiot*.

I didn't like the appearance of the officer who had captured me, so I gave him some back-chat. The soldiers he commanded very properly objected to this, and as I was marched down the road with one of them on either side of me and a third bringing up the rear with a drawn revolver, the man behind me fired at my heel — merely to frighten me, I believe. At the same moment the soldier on my left spun round, threw up his arms and collapsed into the ditch. The soldier who had fired the revolver dashed wildly about the road, shrieking with despair. I had given a lift to a little hunchback with a Red Cross armlet, and he ran up, and having forgotten his first-aid, began to say an Act of Contrition into the dying man's ear. He must have forgotten that too, because he said the Act of Faith instead. I pushed him aside and opened the man's collar and tunic, looking for a wound. At that he opened his eyes and said 'F—— you!'

Then he rose with an air of wounded dignity, picked up his rifle and fell into step again.

A respectable middle-aged writer with his wife and friend, we cycled on in the afternoon light while I tried to identify the cottage where I had been imprisoned. I remembered that it was a little off the road with a yard before it, then filled with captured transport including a charabanc from Waterford and some military lorries. The enemy officer proved to be a charming fellow, quite different from his second-in-command who had captured me. He ordered dinner for us, but I couldn't eat it. Is there anything more humiliating for a romantic young man than to be made prisoner on the very first day of war? He understood that too, and promised to get me a bottle of whiskey at the first pub we passed. But we never got back. Just as he gave the order to start, while the lorries and cars were roaring, and I and the other prisoners were mounting into them, they were swept by a sudden blast of machine-gun fire. Our front-line troops had come back from Mass!

Within, the farm-house grew dark as the windows were barricaded. Some fool put a bucket of pitch on the window-sill, and the first blast of machine-gun fire blew it down on the head of my driver who was lying against the wall. The enemy officer explained in a quiet voice that there was to be no surrender till the last shot was fired. He whispered to his second-in-command that one of their party had been killed upstairs. I passed on the news to encourage the others. The second-in-command sang 'You Called me Baby Dear a Year Ago' in a tuneless voice. There was a deaf man beside me who couldn't understand what had happened. I had to shout it into his ear. He then fell asleep on my chest. At the beginning all the cars and lorries had been roaring. One by one, as the petrol gave out or a bullet caught the engine, they stopped; then during a lull in the firing I noticed the silence. Some of the soldiers started to pass me clips of ammunition until my pockets were loaded. They were tired of it by now.

The enemy officer showed great bravery and presence of

mind. He moved about from room to room, encouraging the men. Coming on to dusk our fellows began to fire rifle grenades. Then the officer fell and a great shout went up. The second-in-command called out to surrender, and I took his handkerchief and rushed out into the yard. It was coming on to dusk and all over the Limerick fields the cattle were roaring to be milked. As I returned to the cottage the enemy officer was lying outside with a priest kneeling beside him. He was spitting out great clots of blood. The bullet had struck him in the mouth. Two other men were bringing the dead lad's body down from the attic. The bullet had gone clean through one nostril and there was a tiny trickle of dried blood across his cheek. Two old people suddenly appeared from under the stairs and asked, 'Is it all over now, sir?'

I felt a little ashamed that I hadn't called at the garage in Charleville. A few weeks after my capture and escape I dropped into Buttevant Military Hospital and saw a man with a bandage about his jaw. It was the officer who had captured me. Later, I heard he had come over to our side, been captured and sentenced to death; made his escape. Now he works in Charleville, but I felt sure if I had called I should have been shy and awkward. Nothing of it all do I remember with pleasure but the conduct of one brave man.

I didn't succeed in identifying the exact farm-house. It was all so long ago that I found I scarcely remembered even what Kilmallock was like. There is a picture in the Dublin National Gallery which shows what Mulvaney saw there a hundred years ago: a street of three-storey fortified Tudor and Jacobean houses which Irish people still properly call 'castles'. That street has now entirely disappeared. A few months before we passed through it the last good example of the Irish fortified house was torn down to make way for a modern cinema. In the ruined gable was a fine stone Tudor fireplace. Nobody in Kilmallock even wanted that. But as the inhabitants are all intensely patriotic (is it not Mr. De Valera's homeland?) they have called the cinema 'The Sarsfield'. In Limerick there is a public-house which with the same appropriateness is called 'The Father Matthew', after the apostle of temperance. At the end of the town there is a dilapidated furniture shed with some metal advertisements for Raleigh bicycles nailed outside it. From the arched doorways you may just be able to identify all that remains of the last of the old Kilmallock houses.

Up a side street we came on the remains of the parish church with a round tower built into it and a beautifully moulded doorway, its bases smothered in a concrete pathway through the filthy graveyard. It looks like a recent victim. Did 'we' burn it? Anyhow, the Protestants have ceased to use the chancel as a parish church and betaken themselves to a nice modern church on the hill. The Catholics have a most impressive-looking Gothic church at the Limerick end of the town, while in a field behind the main street, on the banks of a little stream which runs through neglected fields, stands the charming thirteenth-century Dominican priory. Two sides of its slender tower have collapsed, but it still makes a delightful picture on the little winding stream with its five-light east window, the long row of lancets in the chancel, and the big clumsy reticulated window in its solitary transept off the nave on the south side. Within, dirty and nettle-grown, the ivy climbing the mullions of the east window, it has the tall narrow tower arch of a Franciscan church and delightful little heads at either side. This was the church that Catherine Fitzgerald knew before she stormed out of Kilmallock in a fury on her way to Carrick. You wouldn't think so now.

To realise what has happened Kilmallock, you need to know Adare, a few miles away. Adare, too, is a Desmond stronghold. There is the same river and the same pastures, the same view of the tower on the river-bank, but at one side of the bridge the Augustinian monastery has been turned into the most charming parish church imaginable ; at the other side, the fine, squat, battlemented tower of the Trinitarian monastery marks the Catholic church, while the ruined Franciscan monastery on the golf-course is so beautifully kept that it is a pleasure to wander about it, to watch the patterns of shadow that the sun makes among the piers or see the tall tower through the intersecting mullions of a ruined window.

It is only there you realise the almost incredible achievement of Kilmallock, the one-time capital of Desmond. At the time Mulvaney painted it, it had, in spite of the ruins, the richest past in Munster. Today it has practically none. The Fitzgerald tombs rot under the open sky within the parish church while the Protestants repair to their new church on the hill, the Catholics to their grand Gothic church ; and all of them, the last of their historic houses demolished, to see Hollywood films in a cinema called after Patrick Sarsfield. One glance at that dying hole, and you can understand the dreariest of Mr. De Valera's political manifestos. With a synthetic religion and a synthetic culture, what is there left but abstractions ?

# ❊ 20 ❊

LIMERICK is without exception the pleasantest town in Ireland. It consists of two towns, the old and the new, but as the new was built about the beginning of the last century, the old has grown almost reconciled to it. In the new town is the pretty Custom House, with its arcade cemented up by some genius from the Board of Works, and a fine long street of Late Georgian which ends, rather feebly, in a frightened double crescent. Shop fronts do less to spoil the street than the Renaissance church in Ruabon brick, and the neo-Clonmacnois one in limestone. Limerick as well as being the pleasantest is also the most pious town in Ireland. Why it should be I don't know, except that it was founded by Danish pirates, whose flaxen hair, blue eyes and bad consciences still walk the streets.

The old town is on an island in the river with the Clare shore joined to it by a bridge, and the wild Clare hills up the river behind it. The bridge is guarded by a great castle with drum towers, over which a row of modern workmen's houses peers with a slightly self-conscious air. On a little hill above it stands the cathedral, not very impressive from any angle, for its blue stone gives it a frosty, virginal air ; its tower is skinny and looks as if it needed love, and its walls are decorated with battlements which distinctly resemble curling papers. When you get nearer, you see that it is almost as broad as it is long, and that no two windows in the fifteenth-century shell bear much resemblance to one another.

It is better inside. In the porch there is a shrine with characteristic Transitional ornament, and when you enter you find yourself in a typical Cistercian church of the twelfth century, with sullen, massive piers relieved at the corners by half-columns, plain exiguous capitals and bases, and plain arches without mouldings. It is a very small church ; four bays below the crossing ; but, even so, it seems to have presented its builders and restorers with insuperable obstacles. For some reason it was extended not in length but laterally, in a series of transepts, and, as the builders stuck to piers instead of columns, one's first impression is not of a void with solids in it but of a solid very inadequately provided with voids.

As in many of the English cathedrals, there are curious passages running through the walls, across the west window and up through the clerestory, as though the principal recreation of the chapter were 'Hide and Seek'. On the south side, the clerestory is relatively normal, but on the north the aisle and transepts have been built higher than the clerestory, which thus opens on either side into the church, and accordingly has had to be railed off in case an unsuspecting visitor might take a header into the nave by mistake. It is only when you have had a really good look at the church that you begin to discover half its peculiarities. For instance, in England the clerestory windows are placed above the head of the arch, where, if the church is vaulted, they do not get in the way of the columns supporting the roof. It wouldn't be Ireland if they were not placed above the piers. But the Limerick masons went one better, for they have put one window over the pier, another over the head of the arch, and very odd and very charming they look with their deep sun-filled splays broken by these black, tapering, Egyptian-looking passages.

The fact is that at Limerick we really struck without recognising it a very interesting architectural backwater Munster had been the centre of the reform movement and the probable source from which Romanesque decoration spread up the Shannon into Connacht. For a hundred years after the Normans the O'Brien and O'Connor country west of the Shannon was little affected by the invasions, and while the Normans of the Pale were putting up regular Transitional and Early English buildings which have all the formal beauty of their kind in England, the masons in the west of Ireland erected churches which, though deeply influenced by what was happening in the

east, are still full of character. They are usually plain, sometimes to the point of ugliness; they are nearly always, to use an
Irishism, 'contrairy', but often, too, they have great brilliance,
and are decorative in an exciting way in which the churches of
the east are not.

Half the charm of English church architecture is its peculiar
individualism, but any charm these Irish churches may have is
entirely due to it, and though Célimène and I began by being
repelled, we found ourselves at last becoming attracted in the
way one is attracted by characters one meets in out-of-the-way
places, men who superficially are all angles and oddity, but who,
as you get to know them, reveal their value. When I try to
explain the charm these churches have for me I think of old
apple trees, gnarled and bent, or of the Border ballads in their
harsh, monosyllabic dialect in which nothing can be said grace-
fully, but whose uncouth accents echo in some moment of crisis
all the chivalry of far-away mediaeval Europe with a passion
that wrings your heart :

> He turned her owre and owre again,
>  O gin her skin was white ;
> I might have spared that bonnie face
>  To have been some man's delight.

In the evening we cycled up the river to Castleconnell. A
countryman directed us. ' Ye will go on through the village of
Cloonlara, turn to the right, and then go on for a mile. Now,'
he added cautiously, ' when I say a mile, it might be a mile and
a half, for a countryman's mile is a long mile.' It was ; the
longest mile I had ever cycled. Castleconnell is a delightful
Georgian spa with its arcaded assembly rooms on the bank
of the Shannon, its charming inn, its rows of demure little
villas. Towards the end of the nineteenth century some patriot
got at them and gave them wrought-iron gates, representing
Irish round towers, harps, wolf-dogs, and the Treaty Stone by
Thomond Bridge, but even these do little more than emphasise
the quiet decorum of the houses behind.

Unfortunately, since then it has been visited by another type of patriot. During Mr. De Valera's rebellion some of the great houses along the river perished; under his government the housebreakers have been gradually accounting for the rest. We returned from Castleconnell along the back road just at sunset. Miles of stone wall which guarded the estate on our right were humped and rent by great clumps of ivy which straddled them and broke their back. We opened a ruined gate and cycled down a shadowy lane which had once been an avenue, and rounded a great mass of buildings which proved to be stables. Suddenly as we reached the stable yard, the sun went out over the wild Clare hills across the river, and we looked up and saw in the yellow light the green, peeling stucco behind a great Ionic front, reflecting like water the last pale gleam of day. It would be impossible to paint that yellow light on the peeling stucco and the dull smouldering of the masses of brick in the gloomy cavern of the house behind, but it was tremendous; as though the sun going down beyond the Clare hills had clenched his fist and shaken it at the porch, and the porch, like some great beast driven to bay, dug its columns deeper into the ground and snarled back at it. ' A man must be stronger than God to build to the west of his house ' goes the Irish proverb, but a man must think himself stronger than Ireland to build that insolent classic front to face the wild hills of Clare.

It must have been an enormous house. Outside we could trace the remains of a sunk garden, but of that nothing remained except a clump of wild daisies among the briars. Behind were acres of magnificent walled garden going wild, wilder I think than anything I have seen elsewhere, or perhaps it was the light which made it seem that the earth was rising to swallow up what remained of the house.

Stumbling in the dusk along the length of the wall, we came on a peculiar mound, almost covered with briars, and now almost unnoticeable in the desolation. There was an opening into it, and in the opening a gate with sentimental shamrocks that dated it as of the same period as the patriotic embellishments of

Castleconnell. The lock was broken; we opened the gate and looked in. Three steps led down into the darkness. I lit my lighter, and the flare showed us three discoloured coffins on a slab under broken glass wreaths. We didn't go further. We returned as we had come, under the great Ionic columns that lost themselves in the night sky. As we went back the little dark lane we came upon an old countryman on his way home.

'Whose house was that?' I asked.

'That was the house of Lord Clare,' he said, stopping. 'He was one time Lord Chancellor of Ireland. You might have heard of him?'

'I did,' said I.

'I saw his photograph knocked down at the auction here. Dressed in his robes and all. That was the greatest sale that was ever in these parts. I was only a boy at the time, but I saw them coming here from all parts, Jews and every sort. It went on for eight days. Maybe you wouldn't believe me, but I saw a cup and saucer — one ordinary cup and saucer — knocked down to Mr. Bannatyne of Limerick for ninety-five pounds. Wasn't that a terrible price to pay for a cup and saucer?'

'It was,' said I.

'And still they said things went for half what they were worth!'

'And what happened then?'

'Then the place was bought by an American and his wife. Nevin was their name. They died and left it to the daughter, but poor soul, she hadn't much brains. Too fond of dancing. She was robbed right and left.'

'Are those the three coffins in the grounds?'

'They are. They left orders to be buried there. Then the timber was sold. When I was a boy all this place was woodland. You might have noticed the wall? Three and a half miles round from the Castleconnell Road to Annacotty Bridge. The timber fetched six thousand; it worked out at about fourpence a tree.'

'And then, what happened?'

'It was burned by the boys during the Troubles. They

thought the military might be going to take it over. I saw it burning. There was a marble staircase that stretched the whole width of the house. It melted in the fire, and the melting lead pouring down on to it from the roof. It was a terrible sight ! That was the finest house in this part of Ireland. There was a walk all round the roof. Often and often I strolled up there in the evening after the house was left empty.'

He described it so vividly that I seemed to see it, the figures of bewildered countrymen walking about it, their shadows thrown across the fields and the red light breaking into the tomb where the three coffins lay, so close that a spark might have caught them.

' A wonder,' said I, ' the people here don't be afraid of going past that vault after dark ! '

' Is it that ? ' he said with a pitying smile which I could feel through the darkness. ' I walk past it at twelve and one every night of my life, and I never saw anything. Ach, sure, that is only the old people's foolishness. Some white thing like a donkey they'd see and think it was a ghost.'

' I dare say,' said I, and yet I felt a bit cheated.

' Sure, what else is it ? ' he said with the conviction of the born rationalist who has at length found out the truth about things from the daily newspaper and the wireless.

I didn't know to be sure. ' I look for ghosts, but none will force their way to me.' I didn't see why black Cromwellian landlords should be able to return and terrify the unfortunate country people whom they had oppressed in life, while sentimental Americans who had returned to the country from which they had sprung should be deprived of the chance. They would have appreciated it so much.

## ⁂ 21 ⁂

A FRIEND in Dublin had told us her experiences of one large house where she was nursing an old lady with a broken leg. The old lady passed the time by writing a very long novel which went on and on and on; and as new characters presented themselves they were immediately sucked into the plot. Each evening she read to Sylvie the chapter she had written during the day. In due course Sylvie appeared in it, and so did the doctor. As the old lady was of a romantic turn of mind, she permitted Sylvie (in the novel) to fall in love with the doctor. Sylvie didn't really mind, because she was enjoying herself enormously with the specialist.

When she wasn't thinking about her novel the old lady allowed her mind to dwell on the past glories of her family, and taunted Sylvie with the fact that she was only a builder's daughter.

'And what was your mother?' she asked one evening. 'A shop assistant?'

'Well, what's wrong with it?' asked Sylvie blandly.

'What's wrong with it? You don't think it's anything to be proud of?'

'I don't see why not,' said Sylvie. 'Anyway, she's as good a woman as you are, any day.'

'Certainly not,' said the old lady haughtily. 'You forget that I am one of the landed gentry.'

'Oh, begor, landed is right,' said Sylvie, who has one of the readiest wits in Ireland; and then she fled for her life, for her patient, broken leg and all, leaped out of bed and followed her with a scissors. Sylvie rushed downstairs and out into the park in her uniform. The rain was pouring. It seemed to her that it was time she packed her bag and went back to town. She was getting bored with the country. She waited till the coast was clear and then tiptoed softly up the stairs towards her room.

There was a sedan-chair on the landing, and as she passed it the door suddenly shot open and out jumped the old lady with the scissors.

Landed is right. After the mediaeval cathedral, and the snug Georgian and the beefsteaks and resiners, going into Clare was like going into a land of skeletons, a cemetery of civilisations. On every road there were ruined cottages, by every ford and gap was a ruined tower, in every village the ruins of a Georgian Big House and a church of any century from the tenth to the nineteenth. Protestant and Catholic, we are as decent a race of people as you are likely to find, but without the black of your nail of any instinct for conserving things.

In the hot summer weather in that wild and beautiful country it began to steal over us with an extraordinary feeling of oppression. We sat on a wall by the roadside to suck an orange. Behind us in the pale-green field, a pale-grey tapering tower rose like an oak from an outcrop of rock, and under it the red and black cattle gathered for shade. We heard music in the distance, and at last a tall, ragged young tramp hove into view round a corner, and marched down the hill towards us, playing a mouth-organ. We watched him in fascination, but he hadn't a glance to spare for us. He passed at the quick march, throwing out his feet and swinging his rags gamely to the tune of ' The Men of the West '— a Connacht tramp, to all appearances — and as the music faded down the road I envied him his mouth-organ.

Bunratty was rather grand in its melancholy way ; tall and dramatic above the low, yellow-washed pub by the hump-backed bridge. At the other side of the road on the hill overlooking the river was the ruin of the parish church. The bridge will be the next thing to go. It is obviously going to get in the way of a grand new concrete road from Shannon Airport. I began to compose a letter to Mr. De Valera in my mind, begging him to remove the bridge for aesthetic reasons. I felt almost sure that would save it.

The castle is a big plain keep in the same style as Carrigtwohill Castle, with four square towers at the angles, and three privies in each tower, and in front a round-arched bridge had been thrown across the gap between the two angle towers, converting it into what looked like an enormous entrance gate or a cathedral front in the manner of Peterborough. Inside there were stucco ceilings in the little chapel and what is called the Earl's Room, and for no visible reason a fertility goddess was exposing herself with the greatest equanimity in a wall near the top.

The view from the roof over all that flat river country was magnificent. Under a high grey-and-blue sky the main road, which crossed the hump-backed bridge at our feet, ran straight across country to the spires of Limerick in the distance. Behind us, all the way back to the blue Clare hills, and before us till it reached the Shannon, which was dominated by the ruined keep of Carrigogunnel, the little river, grey with mud, shuddered luxuriously as it performed Samson and Delilah curves through the soft silt, and the mud had risen and covered all the river meadows where the red cattle were lying asleep in the heat of day, giving the whole landscape an indescribably mournful tone.

Our next halt was at Quin, a pleasant village with a ruined parish church and a ruined abbey cheek by jowl with a new parish church. We unpacked the Travelling Kitchen in a grassy spot under the old bridge, and sent Géronte off to look for boiling water. We hadn't fully realised Géronte's views on boiling water till we saw him slinking off with his head down and the can behind his back, making a bee-line for the pub. The poor man was afraid the publican would catch him *in flagrante delicto* with a cup of tea.

The abbey was more nearly complete than anything we saw outside Headford, and was merely waiting for a roof to be the sort of parish church that any cleric with taste would dream about. It was built between the four angle towers of a Norman castle at a time when the Clare men had the Normans where they wanted them, and was designed on the plain and simple lines of the time : a long, narrow, rectangular church with an excruciatingly narrow chancel arch like a lancet window gone wrong, and a tall, tapering tower cockaded with battlements.

It is the Irish equivalent of Perp, and like a lot of Perp it has a slightly mass-produced air, while there are certainly more graceful things in the world than the intersecting mullions of that east window; but to make up for it the irregular battlementing of the tower gives it an enchantingly irresponsible air quite different to the sentimentality of the usual Franciscan tower, and in the afternoon light the fine moulded west door framed the soaring chancel arch and the east window in a splendid perspective of shadows.

Except for its tower which has been improved to death, the Franciscan abbey in Ennis is an earlier and far finer example of the style — need I add that the Franciscans have built themselves a new church round the corner? The first time we came there a little window over the west door caved in and crashed on to the pavement at our feet. Unless, like Pompey's statue, it had actually spouted blood it could hardly have expressed its plight more dramatically.

Then began the well-known Irish game of Find the Key. Denis in the Old Ground told us we might see the caretaker in a pub called Considine's near the Queen's Hotel. So we went to Considine's.

'He wasn't in this morning. He's working.'

'Where is he working?' said I.

'He's drawing for a builder called Pat Smith. He passed a couple of times this morning. If you stand at the corner you'll be bound to see him — a ginger-haired man with an ass and cart.'

So we stood at the corner, looking up and down the road. There was a ginger-haired man driving a trap, and a little boy with an ass and cart, but neither of these was Mr. Fitzgerald. A young man came out of the pub.

'If ye went to the end of the road, ye'd be likely to see him,' he said. ''Tis up there they're building.'

So away with Géronte and myself to the end of the road, but they hadn't seen the caretaker. The light was fading and the abbey looked tantalisingly beautiful in spite of the tower. I went up to a Council worker who was trying to do something to a hose.

'Is it Dykie Fitz?' he cried. 'He's drawing for Pat Smith up in Chapel Lane.'

'And where is Chapel Lane?' I asked.

'At the other end of the town, beyond the O'Connell Monument.'

We returned through the long, snaky main street and finally found Chapel Lane with some Jacobean chimney-pots on a house at its corner. There was no sign of an ass and cart in it. Two men were working on the roof of a house and they peered over the edge at us.

'Is Pat Smith there?' we shouted.

'He's away at his dinner.'

'And where the hell is Dykie Fitz?' (By that time we were calling Mr. Fitzgerald by his nickname.)

'He's just after going down the town with the ass and cart.'

We set off for the abbey again by the back road, and when we had gone a few hundred yards we saw a man coming towards us with an ass and cart.

'That's an ass and cart anyway,' said I.

'It's coming in the wrong direction,' said Géronte hopelessly. 'Wouldn't you think they'd leave the bloody key with the guards?'

'The man has ginger hair,' said I, carefully scrutinising the back of his neck as he passed us.

'There's nothing but straw in the cart,' said Géronte in the tone in which he criticises the Government.

'By God,' said I, making a dash after him, 'he has builder's overalls on! That's Dykie Fitz.'

But it was worth it. Dykie keeps the church tidier than most of his tribe, and even if he does stable the ass there, the ass does less damage than some of his who have passed public examinations and landed Government jobs. The place is rich in sculptural detail. At either side of the chancel arch are a St. Francis and a Man of Sorrows. The stone-mason was awfully good at dripstones — grandda had taught him all about them — and when he came to do the St. Francis he chose the nearest appropriate dripstone head, and then attached a body to it. He wasn't good at bodies — grandda hadn't shown him how to do them; but anyway, his statues, exposed to the weather, will not last long. In a room off the chancel were the fragments of a splendid carved tomb which two intelligent labourers could put together again in about three days. Built into a modern tomb in the chancel and half eaten away by rain, were the five panels of a fine fifteenth-century altar-piece; a stone copy of the alabaster altar-pieces common in England at the time. It is the only example left in Ireland; possibly in the United Kingdom. I began to compose another letter to Mr. De Valera in my head.

This time the line to be taken was rather different. One owned up that the infernal thing was a work of art, but suggested that it might make a pleasant decoration for a villa garden and offered to buy it. The price was a crucial question. I first thought of five shillings a panel, but then I realised that the panels of the Betrayal and Entombment were rather smaller than the others, and that it wouldn't do to overlook the fact. Yes, I thought; five shillings for the large, and three and sixpence each for the small panels will look like a reasonable offer. Otherwise one might be suspected of facetiousness.

The evening light breathed on the panels and brought out the rotting figure of Christ in the Flagellation, and my heart turned sick at the irony. Outside the church a father and son were coming down the main street with linked arms, each sucking a ripe tomato. They were rather drunk. We came on a house with a tablet above its door. It had been destroyed by the Black and Tans and the plaque had been inserted to commemorate its restoration. ' We arise to complete our labours', it said. I glanced down the street after father and son. The house was a pub, and there was no doubt about the labours.

A man would need a mouth-organ.

## 22

NEXT morning when we woke we saw a sheet of gold which filled the lower half of our bedroom window and thought it was a lake, but when I jumped up I found it was the sky, and the lake lay beneath us, a brilliant sky-blue under the limestone hills, all powdered with white as though it were the middle of winter.

A short distance away, with a blue lake at its door and the pale, bumpy limestone hills behind, we came upon Dysert O'Dea church. As we came up the little path from the road we gave a whoop, for there was a real stunner of a Romanesque door, and since we had never heard of it, never seen a photograph of it, it came on us like a thunderbolt. That is one of the pleasures of church-hunting in Clare ; a discovery, if you make one, is likely to be all your own.

At one time Dysert must have been a very rich monastery indeed, because the gaga west window was built of carved stones in half a dozen different styles which must have come from other doors and windows, and even the doorway in the south side of the church looked rather as if it might be the remains of a big ornamental door in the manner of Clonfert. However about that, there was magnificent stone-cutting all up the jambs and along the arch stones which the morning light flooded with shadow. But the unforgettable thing was the row of masks amongst the beakheads round the hood — an unlikely enough position for both. There was not the least trace of character in the proud and melancholy faces with their strongly marked Mongolian features, but neither was there anything of the deliberate distortion which you find in practically all Irish literature and most Irish art. It reminded us again that all art in the European sense is an enquiry into the nature of reality, and that whenever Ireland moved closer to Europe, as she did in that century of the abortive reform movement, the approximation to reality began, and that when later she drew apart again, she reverted to pattern.

We wasted a roll of film on it, but it was well worth it. The *Irish Press* poster in the village announced 'Noted Clareman Laid to Rest', and when I enquired for films I was told that it was only eleven o'clock and the chemist wasn't up yet. A little girl offered to go up and see him, and she came back a few minutes later with the keys of the Medical Hall. There was a little boy standing at the shop door, and, in one of those moods of idiotic amiability which afflict us all at times, I asked him what his name was. He told me his name was Willie Hynes and that he was just after getting up. He seemed to think I ought to congratulate him.

Then a door opened up the street and a shopkeeper came out without collar or tie and began to remove his shutters. First he looked at the sky, and then at me, and then he looked at the sky again. He seemed to think that one or other of us must be in the wrong. The little girl brought me back the films.

'How much is that?' said I.

'I don't know,' she said. 'I'll have to go up and ask the chemist.'

It was a nice restful place, and as we cycled out I read the poster again and decided that the noted Clareman wouldn't note much difference.

The road went on through hard, bumpy country of rounded hills and hollows, with little round lakes as blue and wicked as a colonel's eye, and brilliant fields where the limestone showed everywhere to the hill-tops as though the sea had withdrawn and left them covered in silver sand. It was lonelier than Connemara at its worst, for by this time every second house was a ruin, and they were not mud cabins but fine stone cottages. In some queer way the unmortared fencing walls with the long limestone slabs laid not flat but fanwise, had a frighteningly prehistoric air. The thatch of the little cottages did not come snugly down about their ears, helmet fashion, as in Waterford, but was shaved away at the edge of the gables, the tops of which were whitewashed. It gave them the appearance of a military haircut.

The limestone grew thicker as we went on, till the hills at either side of us were like great blue heaps of cinders in the sunlight. At the crossroads by Corcomroe Abbey there were more cottages in ruins, and they made me so curious that, when we went up to one of the cottages to ask for hot water, I enquired about them from a man with a horse and cart who was standing outside. He looked like a man in the last stages of heart disease.

'You see,' he whispered eagerly through his blue lips, preparing a grand history lesson in case we might be English, 'there was a class of people in the old days called landlords.'

'Oh, so they were evictions!' I said, cutting him short. Irish history always sounds to my ears like the hard-luck story that preludes the touch. We went into the cottage. A chicken with its throat slit was lying by the door, and the whitewashed thatch, yellow with turf smoke, bulged down through the stumps of trees that served for couplings, looking for all the world as if it were limestone too. We both took to the woman of the house at once, and I was even prepared to discuss Irish history with her. I was still curious about that horrible desolation.

'Those must have been shocking evictions round here,' I said.

'Where?' asked the woman in astonishment. 'What evictions?'

'All those ruined houses we met at the road,' said I. 'The man with the horse and cart outside told us they were evictions.'

'He should have more sense,' she said angrily. 'There were no evictions. 'Tis lonesome country, and the young people leave it and the old people die. 'Tis happening still.'

She was right. It was lonesome country, and you could see it by her eagerness when we offered her the daily paper with the report of the noted Clareman being laid to rest.

I do not know why we were bored by Corcomroe Abbey.

The photographs I took at the time suggest that it is an interesting example of the very type of Transitional architecture which we later learned to like. We were even bored by the Conor O'Brien tomb in the chancel which some of our friends admire, and I regret now that we didn't study it more closely, for it has since been smashed by some young hooligans attending a funeral there. But bored we were till we reached the main road by Bell Harbour and saw the view across Galway Bay. By the edge of the sea one lone wall of a fortified house stood up within its battlemented bawn, and through its ruined mullions you could see the Muckinish peninsula which stretched out anglewise till it died in the blue waters. It was no more than a couple of fields high, a patchwork of brown and grey and green, and beyond it Galway and the Twelve Benns lay flat along the horizon, painted as blue as the water, while the little whitewashed cottages that stabbed their flanks with a flaky brightness, looked like little waves tossed up from the bay.

As we mounted the Corkscrew we looked back at the sea, framed in the limestone valley behind us. To the east the land went down in four folds, terraced in the hard, bumpy line of limestone until it flattened itself out in the sea at Muckinish, and the light hit each fold in turn, turning it cinder-bright under the faint opal of the sky, lifting it softly out of the landscape like a sleeper's breast which rose and fell at every breath. Here, the light is the very breath that fills the lungs of the landscape.

Then we slid downhill into the sleepy little village of Kilfenora, with its ugly little Protestant church cut out of the nave of the old cathedral, in the most appallingly filthy graveyard, which seemed to be absolutely littered with bits of high crosses being used as gravestones. If Irish Catholics had ever shown the slightest interest in the architecture of their own churches, one could afford to be furiously angry with the dog-in-the-manger attitude of the Church of Ireland which deliberately cuts its churches to fit its congregations and restores or even rebuilds a small portion of a big church and then allows the rest to drop into ruin. Kilfenora may perhaps be forgiven since for many years it has been poised on the verge of extinction, and kept going only by the faith of its rector. Up to a short time ago it had a congregation of one solitary Protestant, and when he died it seemed the end had come. Then it attracted two new worshippers from neighbouring parishes, and when we saw it, was flourishing again.

At the same time, it is doubtful if any civilised country would have allowed 'Dearly Beloved Roger' to leave unroofed such a window as the east window of Kilfenora. It was a Transitional triplet, and it was the first time we noticed the tendency to turn the whole east wall into a decorative framework for the window. The mason, an excellent one, seems to have been a bit of a joker. One of his capitals, a fine formal bit of work, was scalloped, but then it looks as if he had a row with the chapter about his pay, for when he came to carve the second capital he saw the flowing line of the scallop as a clerical surplice, and carved a whole group of priests with smug, supercilious, clerical faces and piously joined hands. (Of course, it may not have been a joke. There is a corbel very like it in the chancel of Killaloe which shows a group of little men in kilts kissing one another — 'An exhortation to brotherly love,' suggests the local antiquarian).

We spent the night in one of the Big Houses, and after supper Géronte dropped out of the sky in his usual Father Christmas manner, and when the talk got on to Big Houses, Géronte in an absent-minded way put his hand in his hip-pocket and took out a pint of whiskey. Octave looked at it with a slightly astonished air as if he wondered what it could be, but then concluded that it was probably something you took out of glasses and silently set about the job of procuring them.

'Tell me,' said Géronte, returning to the Big House we had been discussing, 'wasn't that the place they roasted the cat?'

'It was,' replied Octave thoughtfully.

'They never did that for you?' asked Géronte.

'Well, no,' said Octave slowly, 'I can't say I ever had a cat roasted in my honour, but I had a houseful of furniture burned.'

'Really?' I said, trying to make my voice sound natural.
'Where was that?'

'That was in B——,' said Octave.

'That was burned since, wasn't it?' asked Géronte by way
of no harm.

'It was,' said Octave archly. 'We burned it.'

'Oh!' said I. (I never did find out exactly why.)

'But that was on a different occasion,' said Octave smoothly.
'At the time I was speaking of I met the Z——'s one day in
town — they were sort of cousins of mine, of course — and we
drove out to B—— together. We had a very nice dinner : soup,
chicken and bacon and lashings of whiskey, but they still felt they
weren't doing me justice. Then they took out all the furniture on
the ground floor and made a bonfire of it in front of the house.'

'But surely the old lady was alive then,' said Géronte.

'She was,' said Octave with great tenderness. 'She enjoyed
it immensely.'

'Then,' he went on after a moment, 'the following Sunday
we were lying in bed, the three of us. There was Ned and Jerry
and myself, and we had a bottle of claret between the three of
us for breakfast. Ned threw the empty bottle out of the window.
It knocked out the centre pane. Then a coach-and-four drove
up to the front of the house. It was the family coach with the
coat of arms on the door. Ned leaned out of the window in his
nightshirt.

'"Take that away to hell out of this," says he. "I'm not
going to drive that thing with less than six horses."

'Ned was the fellow who got into the papers afterwards,
wasn't he?' asked Géronte, determined on elucidating the
family chronicle for me.

'He was,' said Octave. 'When he got mixed up with the
Sultan. Poor Jerry was killed afterwards in an aeroplane crash.'

'His ghost is still seen round the house,' said Octave's lady.

'Oh!' I said again.

'So in due course,' continued Octave, 'back came the coach
with the six horses — six plough horses, whoever gave them or

wherever they were got. Ned and Jerry and myself got up in front. I remember that I was wearing court dress with a mackintosh and a sword. There was a farm-hand behind in the footman's place with a sword in one hand and a dinner-gong in the other, kicking up hell's delights, and two other farm hands inside with a two-gallon keg of whiskey between them. Ned drove. The horses went at a terrible lick ; they were more or less compelled to, since, as you may remember, the road from B—— is all downhill, and there happened to be no brakes on the coach. We arrived in C—— just as Mass was finishing, and when the people heard the hullabaloo they rushed out, and soon we had the whole congregation following us. Then, as the parish priest found himself all alone in the church, he got a bit curious too, and out he belted in full canonicals. It was soon after that that the seat fell out of the coach and the two farm hands were trotting inside.

'It was a great day, a great day ! It was dark by the time we got home, and as we got down off the box Ned said, "I want a tenants' ball tonight." However the news got round there was a ball. They came in their hundreds, a few that were tenants, and a great many more that were not. One of the girls I was dancing with looked at my court dress and said, "Wisha, sir, what regiment are you belonged to ?"'

A year or so later Géronte, Célimène and I were sitting in a pub with some friends with whom we had been church-hunting, and Célimène told the story of a mysterious stranger accompanied by an Indian lady who had descended upon our little town in the east of Ireland. He had bought a boat in which to cross the Atlantic, and taken lessons in navigation from an old captain in the town. The whole town came out to see them off. The old captain begged the mysterious stranger to take a pilot with him out of harbour but he refused. So away the little vessel chugged one fine day ; as she reached the bar she stood almost on her stern and then a great cheer burst from the crowd as the stranger turned to wave his cap to them.

Géronte waited till she had done.

' Remember the family coach in B—— ? ' he asked gently.

' Yes,' we said in surprise.

' Remember Ned that got mixed up with the Sultan ? '

' Yes.  What has that to do with it ? '

' That was Ned.'

## 23

WE left the main road before reaching Gort to plunge into the Burren country by Lough Bunny. Kilmacduagh did not look very much as we drew near it ; it was only from the Gort road that we could look back and see the mighty picture it made, on the long slope of hill with the little farm-house and field of young corn ; the mullioned windows of the cathedral and the pale-grey shaft of the belfry rising into the sky above the bushy, windy country under Slieve Aughty. The cathedral itself is a dull enough building, and so are the little churches round it, but far down in the hollow we found a real little gem in the ruins of Hynes' Church.

This is a very simple church in the Transitional Clare style, with very classical-looking coign-shafts at either side of the chancel. Inside, it is just as beautiful though very plain ; two narrow lancets, each not much more than six inches in width with a very deep splay and hood. The chancel arch is a daring conception which didn't quite come off, for the thin clustered shafts are far too high to leave room even under a high-pitched Irish roof for anything more than a segment of an arch, and, of course, the arch-stones have collapsed.

In Gort we went to see Lady Gregory's house for old time's sake, and it was as well we did, for a few months after the Land Commission of the Irish Government sold it to a Galway builder for £500 as scrap. I was always terrified out of my wits by the old lady, but somehow I feel she deserved rather better than that of the country to which she had given a theatre. We had a meal, sitting on a wall in Drumcree, a little tenth-century church miles from anywhere with a door that might have been taken there from Lincoln Cathedral, so perfect is its Early English detail. And then late on a summer's evening we cycled into Galway — and decided we must cycle out of it first thing in the morning.

I don't know what it is about Galway that affects me like that. I have been there a score of times, and always got out of it as if the devil were at my heels. Once when I was unwillingly spending a night there, the rain set in early and continued in fits and starts. I went for a walk along the sea-front when the rain-clouds stretched from the west over the town in great purple arches like a ruined cloister. Then darkness came. There were ' amusements ' (God help us !) in the Square : a few tents that sheltered some gaming tables and electric bumpers, and in the sizzling white light farmers with very long upper lips fished out big cloth purses from their trousers pockets and cautiously laid their sixpences on the Harp, Crown and Feather. The loud-speaker was blaring out dance music. Beyond the theatrical greenery, lit by the flares, the Square was black and wet and full of the noise of falling rain.

Then the dance music stopped. Voices, as they do in the intervals of music, grew silent, and nothing was to be heard but the bump of the little electric cars. Then after a few bars of introduction a fruity Italian tenor began *La Donna e Mobile*. God speaking to Moses from the mount couldn't have given him a greater shock than I got then. I had a curious hallucination : that the tune was shaped like a pyramid, and the pyramid was all lit up from inside, each face glowing with a different colour. It began to revolve, faster and faster till the different colours chased one another and finally blended into one. It was like a gorgeous glowing peg-top and God the Father somewhere above, flaking it with His mettle. I hurried away for fear I might break the enchantment, and up the stairs to my bedroom I passed a row of tipsy figures sprawled against the wall and banisters. From my window I saw a sea of roofs and the sil-houette of a church tower with four crosses on it against the last dull dregs of woodbine-coloured light, beneath black knots of weeping cloud.

Next morning, after one quick glance at St. Nicholas', probably the best of the remaining Irish parishes churches, we headed off towards Oughterard. It was showery, typically Connemara weather. Sometimes for long spells everything went black out and the mountains disappeared entirely behind a wall of rain. Then came a curious feeling of suspense, and suddenly the hillside on our right began to glow, a single chalky glimmer like the spotlight in a theatre. The chalky spot moved; it flashed upon the road, and, in the bare brown fields at the other side, black-and-red cows were cut out of the landscape with extraordinary vividness. It swept across the margin of a lake and turned it a brilliant blue. The mountains still remained invisible and the sky above them was streaked with a muddy brown stain, but even as one looked at it the veil of rain began to grow transparent, dazzling, spinning threads of it, and behind it we saw, not so much the mountains themselves but the shadow of clouds on the mountains; and then, as the lighting was stepped up and the cloud shadows grew clearer, you saw, in faint blue pencil lines like veins, the planes of the mountain, with silver flashes that crossed them from torrents in flood. It was wonderful, theatrical to the last degree, but lonesome beyond belief.

We stopped on the way for a drink. I wanted Célimène to meet the publican whom I had taken a great fancy to years before when I first cycled that way. When I went into the pub that first day there was another man inside. He was sitting against the back wall with a pint in his fist, and was obviously dying with curiosity about me. As I sipped my stout I could feel his eyes boring through me from behind. At last he couldn't bear it any longer, and it burst from him like a cry of pain.

'You'd be an artist, I suppose?'

'Well, well, well!' said the publican in annoyance, taking down a bottle and dusting it. He had obviously been waiting for it too, and it made him crosser when it came. 'There's a question!'

'Well, what's wrong with it?' asked the customer truculently.

'It's an ignorant question,' the publican replied in a dry, contained sort of voice, 'an ill-bred question.'

'Sure, I meant no harm,' the customer protested, beginning to wriggle at the contempt in the other man's voice.

'I'm surprised at you,' the publican went on in the same dry, businesslike tone. 'Astonished at you! I'd say nothing if it was a poor, ignorant, mountainy man, but an educated man like you — a poet!'

'And is he a poet?' I asked, seeing the drift of the publican's comments, which were intended less to reprove the poet for his bad manners than to enlighten me about his talents — a subtle man!

'He is,' said the publican despondingly, 'and wouldn't you think he'd have better manners?'

'Sure, man,' said the poet, 'don't you see 'tis the way I'm so quickened with drink? Why do you be always at me when you know I'm so sensitive? I'm your best customer, and you're always taunting me.'

'You're my most consistent customer,' said the publican sharply. ''Tisn't quite the same thing.'

'That's a nice point,' agreed the poet. 'I must meditate on that.'

'You might,' said the publican caustically. 'And here's another point for you as you're about it.' He was still busy with his bottles, and hadn't as much as an eye to spare for me. 'Supposing, for the sake of argument, and not by way of looking for information, supposing, I say, this gentleman wasn't an artist but a writer, what would he say when he was writing a book about it after but that the people of this place had no manners?'

Oh, a *very* subtle man!

'I'm sorry, I'm sorry,' said the poet hastily.

'You'll have a drink with me anyway,' I said in Irish.

'I will,' said the poet.

After a while he broke into English again, an elevated style of English that was suitable for a poet.

'When I'm with a mountainy man,' he confessed, 'I talks English as common as dirt, but with an educated man like you I always speaks educated English.'

'Can't you say one of your poems for him?' said the publican.

'I couldn't,' said the poet coyly.

'You're ready enough to say them when you're not wanted,' commented the publican remorselessly. 'Why couldn't you?'

'I'd be too shy,' said the poet.

'Too conceited,' added the publican.

'Now you're wronging me,' the poet said passionately. 'I'm not conceited. I'm full of humility.'

'Well, well, well,' commented the publican again.

'And what's wrong with that?' asked the poet challengingly. 'You know what the doctor said about me. He said I was too intellectual.'

'There's humility for you!' said the publican, shaking his head as if despairing of human integrity. 'You're my best customer and you're too intellectual! Well, well!'

'But damn it, man, when I'm only quoting!' cried the poet.

'Go on and say a poem for the man,' the publican said irritably.

'All right, all right,' bawled the other indignantly. 'Anything to take your tongue off me.'

He rose and stood before me, looking first at the ceiling for inspiration and at the floor for recollection.

'The match I wrote this poem about,' he said confidentially, laying hold of me by the lapel of the coat, 'was a football match. 'Twas played in the town of Galway. I wasn't there myself. I imagined it.'

'Stand back from your audience,' said the publican coldly.

But the poet had no intention of standing back. He held me tightly by the coat and fixed his two eyes on mine as if he were trying to hypnotise me, and then began to speak his poem in the traditional style, half chant, half patter. The warmer he grew the tighter he held me, till at last I was leaning back from him while the publican impatiently begged him again to 'stand back from his audience'. I do not remember more than a few lines of the poem. One was 'I am not one for fiction, no, nor for camouflage' which rhymed with a line describing the people 'in a rage', but there was one verse which ended up in a startling way 'as in wild earth a Grecian vase':

> A might cry of triumph then rose up from the crowd,
> And went right up to Heaven and up through Shelley's Cloud.

A farmer interrupted us, coming in on business.

'You'll have a drink?' said the poet.

'I will,' said the farmer.

So he called for a pint, drank it and went off, almost without bidding us the time of day. The publican watched him closely and nodded with a grim smile at the poet.

'You'd ask that fellow to have a drink,' he said, 'and you wouldn't ask the gentleman here to have a drink.'

'Ah, he's an old neighbour,' said the poet, who was obviously a little put out himself.

'A damn good neighbour he is too,' said the publican ironically. 'This gentleman stood you a drink, and you wouldn't even ask him if he'd have another. You stood that fellow a drink, and he just walked out and left you there — and serve you damn well right!'

'But I tell you the man is a neighbour,' said the poet passionately, and it was quite clear that he hadn't the slightest intention of offering me a drink even if my tongue was hanging out for it. 'If a cow of mine got sick in the morning, 'tisn't to this gentleman I'd be coming for help. Why do you be always at me when you know I'm so sensitive?'

'You have a damn thick hide,' growled the publican, 'to take a drink from the man and not offer him a drink back, and then offer a drink to another man entirely.'

Some time after I met a man who identified the publican from my description of him. According to him the publican had spent the greater part of his life out of Ireland. He also added, which may explain his attraction for me, that he had left Ireland a young man, knowing every line of Raftery's songs

147

by heart, and returned a middle-aged one, still with every line by heart. The pub when we revisited it was just the same, but a little girl served us, and there was no sign of the publican or the poet. I was sorry for that. It was one of these little scenes that stick in a man's memory for life.

## 24

BUT as we cycled on through Leenane, Delphi and Doolough, I found that the magic of Connemara is now for younger men —'I cannot pay its tribute of wild tears', as Yeats says. In those days it had seemed the height of romance. There was scarcely a pub you dropped into but someone was there ready to talk, like the old man who had once assisted at an operation. 'It was on a post-mistress here that married an old devil of an Orangeman, and then didn't she get a growth in her liver. But the foolish man was so fond of her that he wouldn't let them take her to Galway for an operation. They had to do it in the house, and her brother, a doctor in England, was wired for to assist. Then, when they had her opened up and had a good look at her, her brother dropped in a dead weakness on the floor. The surgeon shouted for me. "Hould that," says he, and I gave wan look at her, reached out my hand to hold whatever part of her he gave me, and then turned away my eyes. They had her skivered across like a sheep.'

But sometimes even then it was the reality rather than the romance that was forced on you, like the day when I went looking for a pub where there wasn't one, and an old countryman, dropping his voice, directed me to a house where there was a decent little woman that he felt sure would oblige me. I had never been in a shebeen before, and when I knocked the door was opened two full inches, and inside I saw first the cocked eye and then the whole visage of the decent little woman that might oblige me. It reminded me distinctly of a butcher's block.

'Good morrow to you, ma'am,' said I in the breezy tone that I thought suitable for a young man with no regard for the law.

'What do you want?' she asked with sour suspicion.

'You'll excuse me, ma'am,' said I, trying to be confidential in the space of two inches, 'but a man I met down the road told me you might be able to oblige me with a drink.'

'With a what?' said she, and with the shock she opened the door another inch or so. 'Oh, my!' she added in a tone of great astonishment and grief, 'what made him say a thing like that?'

'Don't ask me, ma'am,' said I, 'but I'm not a Civic Guard, if that's what you're thinking.'

'Oh,' she cried, opening the door just wide enough to allow her own dumpy figure to emerge, 'what is it to me whether you are or not? Where would I get drink?'

At the same time she gave a look up and down the road to see if there was anybody following me and then looked at myself again. I suppose I must have had an innocent sort of face for a policeman.

'All the drink I have,' she said, 'is one bottle of stout that I got for my own dinner, because I'm not well and the doctor says I must drink stout. If that'd do you, you'd be welcome.'

'That would do me fine,' said I, and she showed me into the darkest, most deplorable-looking little parlour with a tiny window, the walls almost papered with photographs and a big mysterious-looking sideboard facing the window. I wasn't well inside before I began to regret it. The decent little woman stood before the sideboard as she opened it, but I had plenty of chance of seeing the array of bottles. The glass was dirty and the stout was flat, but indeed, no flatter than I was. She sat in front of me with her two hands folded limply on her lap, studying me with the greatest attention. She didn't ask me if I were an artist; she probably took that for granted.

'Had you a long journey?' she asked.

'Well, I've come from Dublin,' said I, trying to tell her as little as possible.

'My daughter was in school in Dublin. That's her picture on the mantelpiece. She was in B—— convent.'

'It's supposed to be a good school,' said I.

It cost a lot of money,' said the decent little woman.

' It's worth it,' said I. ' I suppose she's left it now ? '

' She is,' said the D.L.W. ' She failed.'

' Oh, dear ! ' said I.

'So then I sent her to Limerick, to L—— Convent,' she went on.

' And did she get on better there ? ' I asked politely.

' No. She failed there too.'

'Oh,' I said, ' you've had a lot of trouble with her, haven't you?'

' I have,' said the D.L.W. without much emotion. ' She's in —— School in Cork. Is that any better, do you think ? '

' I should say it's a very good school,' said I. ' I've been there a few times. Does she like it ? '

' I got a letter from her a couple of days ago,' said the D.L.W. ' It seems she thinks she's going to fail there too. Education costs a lot of money.'

' It certainly does,' said I. Even shebeen-keepers have their troubles .

' You wouldn't know the head mistress there ? ' asked the D.L.W.

' As a matter of fact, I do, a little,' said I.

' What sort of woman is she ? '

' A very nice woman,' said I.

' I suppose she'd have a lot to say to it ? '

' Oh, good Lord, no,' I cried. ' The head mistress has nothing to say to things like that. The examinations are set and supervised from Dublin, and the teachers know nothing about them.'

I looked at her, and it was revealed to me that she hadn't an idea under Heaven what I was talking about. I found it rather upsetting. Maybe, after all, I found myself thinking, the woman might be right. A decent little woman who makes a living outside the law would know a great many things that would be hidden from artistic chaps like me.

' I suppose it costs a lot ? ' she asked with her mouth set.

' What ? ' I asked with a start.

' Getting a girl through her examinations.'

'If you paid a hundred pounds you couldn't do a thing like that,' I said with all the conviction I could muster, but once more when I stole a look at her I realised that she didn't believe a word of it. She was wondering if she could trust me with money to bribe the head mistress for her. I bolted. The air outside seemed marvellous, but whatever the deuce that woman knew about life, she seemed to know a great deal more than I did.

It is all there, my youth, a blessing go with it, but I cannot recapture its magic. That is why I remember so very little of our journey till we came to Westport in the dusk and saw the Octagon, the best public square in Ireland if it weren't for what the inhabitants have done to the charming proportions of roof and windows ; and the octagonal Glendinning monument looking like a Rodin in the dusk — except for the corrugated-iron urinal tacked on to its base. There is no doubt of it, we Irish were never intended to live in towns. But we haven't yet succeeded in ruining the mall with its charming Georgian houses and its ravishing little bridges with their wide wings which span the stony bed of the water-course. Westport is one of the most gracious of Irish towns, but it gave us a poor welcome. I had expected the waiter in the hotel to greet me like a long-lost brother. When I had last been there we had had long conversations. His theme was human folly. He approved of cycling but frowned on pedestrianism. 'Last year,' he said, 'the foot was prominent, but this year people seem to have got some sense. I see no sense in walking. I once saw a photograph of the Highland Light Infantry after three days' marching on Salisbury Plain.' And when I asked him about a hotel he had replied with an indescribable air of contempt, 'A fishing hotel. You look round you and everywhere you see salmon and trout in glass cases, but when you ask for a bit of fresh fish for breakfast — sorry, we haven't any.'

But he entered the dining-room just as Célimène and I had taken our seat by the window and motioned us with a wave of his napkin to a miserable table at the back. We protested, but he said ' Laid ' in a pained tone. It was impossible to convince Célimène that he and I had once been bosom friends. She was certain I had been boasting. Whether it was that meditation on human folly had embittered him, or that he disliked Célimène, he rejected all my overtures, and she grew more and more furious at his coldness.

We cycled south on a perfect Connacht day with grey skies and a west wind blowing. Croagh Patrick was on our right, a cone of the purest crystal, standing on the edge of the pale-green fields or reflected in dark-brown, oily bog pools which quivered without breaking its image. A short mile off the main road we came upon Ballintubber Abbey, and rubbed our eyes because there was a roof on it.

' This must be a Protestant church,' said Célimène.

' It looks like it,' said I. As we circled it round the east end we found a beautiful triplet of windows with round arches, Transitional ornament and capitals with queer crabbed designs which looked like stiff-leafed foliage put through a Celtic mangle. Inside the sacristy which was open there was an appalling fifteenth- or sixteenth-century tomb (much admired by our guide-book) in which the hair and beard of the golliwog apostles went off into spirals in the manner of eight-century illuminations.

The beautiful chancel, terribly weathered, might have been that of one of the great Cistercian abbeys, with the groining taken off brackets like those of Knockmoy. The builders had thoroughly enjoyed themselves over the new freedom of early Gothic, and the transept chapels alternated fat round and lean pointed arches — an odd effect, rather like Mutt and Jeff, but excellent. Then we realised the existence of the horrible statue of the Sacred Heart and the cheap Stations of the Cross, and saw that it wasn't Protestant after all. But what the blazes was it ? Only the transepts were roofed, and the main door opened on a long, unkempt and ruined nave. There was obviously some sort of story here.

As we left the church I asked a countryman how long it was since the abbey had been roofed. He thought it was about thirty years. Something began to stir in my memory which did not come to the surface for a very long time. Was it in George Moore I had read of a priest who had had some plan for restoring the ruined churches of Ireland, and beginning with his own, had been stopped half through the work by Archbishop MacEvilly. MacEvilly is still a name of terror in the west of Ireland. He was a strict old disciplinarian, and whenever he heard that a few of his unfortunate curates had started a card school, would say grimly, ' Gimme me pin till I schatther 'em.' ' Bring me me pin till I suspend Father Tom,' he would roar when one of his parish priests got too fond of the bottle. And wasn't there a whole Mayo village, excommunicated during his lifetime, which welcomed in his successor with brass bands and torchlights ?

I had it ! There was an old pisherogue which said that the day Ballintubber was re-roofed would be a black day for the Stantons, and the MacEvillys, as everyone knows, are a branch of the Stantons, and with all the good-will in the world towards the Almighty, the great Archbishop of Tuam had no intention of offending the fairies. The roofing of Ballintubber stopped. I was glad we had turned back before the wilds of Mayo. The fairies don't like architecture. That may be why there is so little of it left.

The only advantage I could see in Ballinrobe was that every shop was also a pub, and Célimène was able to buy herself a pair of sandals and drink a pint simultaneously, an amenity impossible in London. But as we left the town by the Clonbur road and turned again into the mountains, the whole countryside lit up. The naked mountains looked magnificent in the evening light ; soused in atmosphere till they were almost transparent ; the little tilled fields humanised the austere and ethereal beauty of the landscape, while the tiny cottages with their doors and gateways, painted a brilliant crimson that ran through the grey air like wine, and their roofs freshly patched with primrose straw, were whitewashed till they shone.

The lake has dropped from round the little island of Inishmain and you can walk across its bed of great flagstones to the tiny monastery church with a crabbed little chancel arch and a pretty east window, obviously by the mason responsible for Ballintubber. We cycled on into the scabby village of Cong and ended up in time for dinner at the Honourable Ernest Guinness' country residence, which has been turned into a hotel. It is a good place to study architecture because the architect had obviously spent a lifetime doing the same. The castellated bridge made even the stream look coy — after all it *was* only a little bog stream — and the sight of the castle and separate keep (pure Hollywood, ivied to the first storey) overwhelmed us so much that we took hands like the Babes in the Wood and walked twice round it before we even found a door. Our bedroom, which had a pet name so that you could call it if it went astray, looked like part of a typist's dream of a honeymoon with a dark man from over the water, for it appeared to be approximately five hundred yards long, with a window overlooking the lake, and the two beds in an alcove you could lose yourself in.

I never go to the pictures but I come out with a feeling of gratitude to the Creator that I am permitted to live in a naturalistic universe. I felt like that coming out among realistic life-sized woods. Among the trees, on the bank of the crystal-clear stream, so still that it might have been enchanted, was the thirteenth-century abbey where in some earlier building Rory O'Connor, last king of Ireland, ended his days. On the edge of the stream, carpeted with wild strawberries, was the monks' fishing hut. Only the east end of the church remains, with a triplet of lancets and a carved north door that with most ingenious clumsiness tries to combine Irish Romanesque decoration with Early English design, but the cloisters are almost complete.

> Darkly grows the quiet ivy,
> Pale the broken arches glimmer through ;
> Dark upon the cloister garden
> Dreams the shadow of the ancient yew—

Rolleston's beautiful poem conveys the whole spirit of the place, but Célimène wasn't interested in Rolleston. She had recognised our old friend of Ballintubber, every capital a complex.   Célimène said it was sexual repression, I said the fairies.

There are no fairies there now.   Whether that is the effect of the Scandinavian church which some public-spirited person built cheek by jowl with the abbey, or of Mr. Guinness' château, I do not profess to say.   But I can maintain the ruins are completely sterilised, and may be visited by the most timid even in moonlight.   'The young eternal river-voices of that western vale' which Rolleston wrote about have no statement to make ; and even though our own night in the hotel was not all it might have been, that was not because we were disturbed by ghosts, but because though Célimène is a very nice girl, she did not go with the architecture.   Greta Garbo and myself would have had a lovely time.

I offer it as a suggestion to students of psychic phenomena that while fairies — witness Ballintubber Abbey — dislike other styles of architecture, they are terrified out of their wits by Victorian Gothic.

## 25

STILL looking back in a dazed state at Mr. Guinness' heroic mansion, I cycled straight into a tree, an accident that embittered every inch of the way to Headford for me, because after it for some reason it was exactly as if I were cycling head on into a gale, and Célimène, who examined my machine and could find nothing wrong with it, decided it was nothing but bad temper. Then I really got bad-tempered, having been so cruelly misunderstood.

By the time we reached Headford pedalling was an agony, and that may have prejudiced me against the friary with the poetic name of Ross Errily, ' one of the most charming of the monastic ruins of Ireland ', said my invaluable guide-book. Admittedly Célimène and I were no longer speaking, a matter which always affects my judgment, but I couldn't for the life of me see how that very commonplace building, of the usual Franciscan type, with the one aisle and transept, a round-arched arcade that was uglier than anything I had ever seen even in a modern church, and the usual dull, dull intersecting mullions, could possibly be called anything except a little horror.

It was a great triumph for me when the garage hand in Headford professed to find something wrong with the gears of my bicycle ; at least it put Célimène in the wrong, and while it was being repaired we sat in the pub opposite and made it up. But when I had paid for the repairs I found the damn thing wouldn't go at all. I invited the mechanic to try it for himself, and he cycled it up and down the main street, returning very much out of breath to admit that it was a bit stiff. And then at the same moment the pair of us noticed that the cable brake had become wound about the handle-bars ! Of such trifles is happiness made: The sun came out, and for the rest of the day things grew better and better.

We weren't far out when I had to stop at a cottage to enquire the way to Annaghdown, just as the door opened and an old man in a black knitted vest came out. He had a knife in his hand which he had come to sharpen on the wall. He listened to my questions and slowly mounted the few steps from his cottage to the road without replying. He made it plain that this was something he could not afford to treat lightly.

'What part of Annaghdown?' he asked at last.

'The abbey,' said I.

He let himself slowly down on the low wall and gave me a long, searching look.

'Do you know anything about it?' he asked by way of being casual.

'No,' said I, a little taken aback.

'Would it be any harm asking,' he went on in the tone of a man abruptly changing the conversation, 'what part of Ireland are you from?'

'None in the world,' I replied cheerfully. 'I'm from Wicklow.'

'Wicklow?' he repeated with a far-away look in his eye. 'Bray, Enniskerry, Arklow.'

'So you were there yourself?' said I, falling straight into the trap.

'I was not,' he replied serenely. 'Rathdrum,' he went on in a meditative tone as though he were recollecting pleasant days he had spent there. 'Lugnaquilla, the Sugarloaf.'

Then he began to draw figures on the wall with his knife. In Ireland you never know what you are letting yourself in for when once you ask the way.

'There's a window in the abbey,' he said like a man starting out of a dream, 'and there's a strange thing about it; a thing no one could ever explain to me. There is a stone in the jaw with a figure of the Lamb of God on it with his legs in the air.'

'Is there, begor?' said I.

'There is,' he said impressively. 'And there is a stranger thing than that. There is a stone in the arch with a fish on it, and he doubled in two, as if you were after making two halves of him with your knife. What explanation would you have of that?' he added sharply.

'I'd have to see it first,' said I.

'There were scholars from all parts there and they couldn't explain it,' he said reprovingly. He didn't think it in the least nice of me to imagine that I could solve a thing like that by my own unaided understanding. 'But I have an explanation for it. I'm a bit of a mason myself and I studied it.' He paused for a moment before entering on the explanation and then went on with another abrupt change of tone. 'The abbey is a fine building. It was built in the sixth century. Am I right?'

'You're right,' I said admiringly. (God forgive me!)

'By St. Finian?'

'St. Finian it was.'

'Of Clonard?'

'The very man!'

'And St. Colum Cille was along with him. Am I right?'

'To be sure you are,' said I.

Then he explained to me exactly why the Lamb of God on the 'jaw' of the window had his legs in the air and why the fish was in two pieces. 'Now, the remarkable thing,' said old Cardinal Logue, describing a statement of Mr. De Valera to the Irish Bishops, 'was that none of their lordships understood one single solitary word that Mr. De Valera spoke, and I only understood one, and that was "Yes", so I took it he meant "No."' Plain metaphysics are difficult enough, but folk metaphysics are the very devil, and Célimène looked first at him and then at me and finally mounted her bicycle.

He wanted to tell me about the cross of St. Bride without e'er a shaft to it, but I had to go. Lough Corrib was lying in a long, bright, sedge-bordered streak between the scarecrow fields; a sedgy, slimy, milky green, unlike anything I had ever seen unless it was the green of mildew or of bile; the old leaky thatch of the sky let through a dribble of light that made the clusters of little cottages look as though they had been dipped in a rainbow, with the colour of turf on the old thatch and of primroses on the new ; the whitewash so brilliant that it turned sky-blue in the shadow, and the golden gables of harvest behind — everything squat and dwarfed amid the pallid lacework of low unmortared walls which traced every hump and hollow of the tiny grey fields.

At the head of the bay was the untidy graveyard with the ruined parish church and the east window of the old abbey in it. The window was apparently brought here for safety, but now the church itself is a ruin, and the cut stones of its windows removed for local purposes, while through the raw gashes in its walls we saw the rocky bay with the blue Connemara mountains behind. The window was of Transitional type, excellent without being exciting, the long slabs laid fanlike across the splay, and then pointed like the top of a paling in a frame of chevron, carved with variations of the usual flower pattern ; and there, sure enough, was one chevron with the Lamb of God on it with his legs in the air, and another with a leaping fish, exactly as old Puzzle-the-World had described them.

Célimène, myself and a starving old sheep-dog made a very nice meal in the ruins of the abbey, where among heaps of Romanesque stones two pilasters of the old west door had been restored. It was a door of the usual heavy Midland type with squat Eastern-looking pilasters, except that here they were decorated down the face with rosettes, an ornament usually reserved for the soffits of archstones.

And then, just as we turned to reach the main road on our way back, who should we see but the Ancient Mariner, sitting on the grass by a wall in wait for us, and two young men sitting beside him, invited there to watch his triumph over the strangers. Strangers are the only chance an intellectual man gets of demonstrating his superiority before the neighbours.

'Did ye see it ? ' he shouted, scrambling to his feet to halt us.

'We did,' I said, dismounting. (Célimène cycled on, but, damn it, I hadn't the heart. Strangers come like Christmas in places like that.)

'And was I right?' he asked, as though there were any doubt of that in his own mind.

'I think,' I said weakly (I feel sure I have English blood in me), 'they carved it like that just to fill the frame better.'

'But didn't you notice the fish?' he exclaimed indignantly.

'I did.'

'And didn't you notice he was in two slices?'

'I did.' (God forgive me!)

'And you'll allow there was Death?'

In a crisis the English blood in me doesn't amount to much and I rush for the nearest air-raid shelter. At that moment I'd have been prepared to allow anything.

'I do, I do.'

'And Separation?' he shouted.

I allowed the Separation as well.

'There was the need for Resurrection?'

'There was.'

That at least justified him before his audience; he let me off the cross of St. Bride without e'er a shaft, and resumed his seat against the wall, his arms folded and his legs stretched out.

'There isn't a man in this place could tell you that, only myself,' he said complacently. 'And I'll tell you a stranger thing than that. There was a certain woman from these parts and her daughter was buried in that graveyard. The woman herself went to live in the town, and nothing would do her only to bring the daughter's body back with her. So she did.

'But the man and the two horses that brought back that body were both struck down. They were — struck down! — and the son and the daughter she had left to her were useless from that day out. The son was simple. I saw him myself with a white hat on his head and a parasol in his hand, and he was that simple, if the rain was pouring from the heavens he wouldn't have the sense to open the parasol.

I thanked him for the information and went on. Célimène, who was taking no chances, was a full half-mile away by this.

## 26

WE set off across country, passing by the abbey of Clare-galway, a really charming Franciscan abbey beside an old bridge and castle on the Tuam road, and came in the heel of the evening to the beautiful Cistercian abbey at Knockmoy. Wherever the Cistercians came, they brought their water-mills, and though the Cistercians are gone the mills remain. The cumbersome wheel turned laboriously as the water cascaded over its bottle-green boards, and the dynamo filled the solitude of the flat, green, silent country with its monotonous clack, while the ruined gable of the church threw back the wind-sharpened light like metal, and its ragged edges were traced against the sky as with a diamond. Inside, it was very plain, very dignified, with a Romanesque triplet in the deep shadow of the groined chancel, and a high arcade which was merely dug out of the thick wall of the nave.

Dark came too soon for our comfort, and, cycling past little cottages whose windows glowed redly, with a pudding-faced yellow moon behind us sliced by cloud, and with a dead weight of rain in the air, we came upon Tuam, stretched in one straight line of lights across the landscape — a whore's ghost of a town. We asked advice of two guards at a street corner, but they gave us small consolation. There was a pig fair next day, they said, and it would probably be hard for us to get a room in a hotel.

Actually it wasn't, and we should have been grateful ; we had had our fill of architecture, such as it was, but the appetite grows by what it feeds on, and after a meal in the big draughty hotel we set out to explore — oh, by way of a little walk before bedtime, of course, nothing more ! Now, the reason we were spending the night in Tuam was because there was a Protestant cathedral which we wanted to see, but the remarkable thing about that walk was that neither of us mentioned the word ' cathedral ', neither being willing to admit that he hadn't really had enough and couldn't bear to wait till morning to see whatever was to be seen. Consequently neither of us could ask the way, so we walked at random in one direction, scanning every gateway we passed till a fresh row of whitewashed cottages and a fresh reek of turf smoke blew on our eagerness like a cold blast from mid-Atlantic, reminding us of Connacht all round us in the darkness; and we retraced our steps with our tails between our legs, thinking what great fools we were to spend a night unnecessarily in a place like Tuam.

' I think it's too soon for bed,' Célimène said mournfully.

' So it is,' said I. ' We'll try another road.'

She did not ask for what. Nature, as the *Cork Examiner* once pointed out, has been bountiful to this country in the matter of beautiful scenery and the supply of fish, but in Connacht there is too much of both, and in me they produce an absolutely ravenous appetite for civilisation. A little is enough to make me feel at home: a carved doorway or a beautiful house, so long as it suggests expensiveness, good manners and adultery; but if I do not get that I am apt to go a little mad. Galway, for instance, gives me hallucinations, and Tuam was like Galway, only worse.

In the watery moonlight we saw a big tower behind a wall of trees, climbed a stile, and walked about a large, ignorant-looking Victorian church. No one could possibly take it for a mediaeval cathedral, though there was a bit of it at the back with over-arching buttresses which struck us as being rather nice. Then we looked at the front again.

' This is surely the *Catholic* cathedral?' said Célimène.

' It certainly looks like it,' said I.

' The guide-book says it's rebuilt in the original style,' said Célimène. ' Is that like the original style?'

' The original style or an original style?'

' It's still rather early,' said Célimène with a sigh.

' We'll try another road,' I said cheerfully.

So we went back again past the market cross and chose another road. We hadn't far to go. There against the moonlight was the tower of another church, and we stopped dead as the last flicker of hope went out.

'I suppose,' I said sadly to a passer-by, 'this must be the Catholic cathedral?'

'That's right,' he said. 'It is.'

'Nature,' I quoted regretfully, 'has been bountiful to this country in the matter of beautiful scenery and the supply of fish.'

Next morning we came down to breakfast when the square was filled with lean men who leant against the walls of banks, and rosy, shiny pigs who trailed their little bits of rope in the silvery sunlight under the old high cross. It must have looked very fine when it was tapered up to its full height, but now the head has been stuck on to a truncated shaft which makes it look as though it were suffering from goitre. The road to the cathedral was lined with red-and-blue creels uptilted at the kerb, framing patterns of rosy bonhams who filled the town with their screeches whenever some dealer lifted one of them out by the tail. On the way we passed a stone-cutter's whose two villa gate pillars had magnificent classic capitals. It raised our spirits a little, for the stone-cutting tradition only lingers where models of some sort remain, as at Cashel and Ardfert.

'This is the twelfth century,' the caretaker declared proudly, pointing to the massive chancel arch. 'This is the Romaness arch.'

It looked extraordinary from that ghastly nineteenth-century nave 'in the original style', because, through the Romanesque triplet of the east window, we had a view of another, Gothic cathedral behind — the little building with the arched buttresses which we had noticed the previous night in the moonlight. The builders of the Gothic church, now used as a chapter-house, didn't like to destroy the chancel of the older church, so they took it in as a west porch, and the nineteenth-century architect reversed the process, so that you now have bits of three different cathedrals strung out in a line with a thin slice of the original one like the roast beef in the sandwich.

The chancel arch itself was most elaborately ornamented, a rather thankless job, because it is such a whopper that it dwarfs the ornament, which anyway is far too finicking. Also, the arch is very worn, the red sandstone shafts have almost lost any shape from being used so long as whetstones. The capitals, if you could call them capitals, had interlacing and flat grotesque heads with ornamental eyebrows, beards and moustaches, all blown out to fill the wide jambs like the figures on playing cards. 'Toby Jug sculpture,' muttered Célimène, not in any carping spirit. Owing to Nature's bountifulness in the matter of beautiful scenery and the supply of fish, all sculpture in Connacht has a tendency to go Toby Jug, and no wonder.

The east window was fine. The splay of the three lights left two narrow shafts, decorated up the face with interlacing, flowers and grotesques, and the ornament encroached on the splay in metal-like bosses like the clasps on an old book. The carving on the hood was slightly bolder, but not enough to remove the impression of intense preciousness. This and not chancel arches was the sort of job that really suited the stone-cutters, for it was not stone-cutting at all, but metal-worker's ornament ; at a few yards' distance it was scarcely discernible ; yet when the lights were switched on over the shabby red altar-cloth and the stonework glowed like ivory under the enormous red chancel arch, it was beautiful enough to take our breath away.

'Thanks be to God,' I said, quoting my grandmother's grace after meals, 'we're neither full nor fasting.' We had had our little bit of civilised life, enough to keep us going until dinner-time at any rate, and we went up the street, looking the bonhams in the eye without a trace of panic. There weren't many of them left. Outside the hotel we were hailed by a pig-buyer with all the delight of a man meeting old school friends in the Sahara. The fat pigs were all loaded on to the Dublin train, and he was paying out on the railway dockets of their owners, who came up to him timidly with all the melancholy of Connacht in their misty eyes. He dealt them out their money ; they counted it, handed him back the luck money, and he put it in his pocket without a ' thank you '.

' Aha,' he said joyously, ' I saw ye in Carrick-on-Suir a couple of weeks ago.'

' That's right,' said Célimène. ' Are you from Carrick ? '

' A better place than where ye are now,' he said.

' How do you find the people here ? ' I asked him. (I am always eager to know the views of people on their neighbours, they are usually so enlightening.)

' Is it them ? ' he exclaimed with a wave of his hand. ' Ach, they're not the same class at all up here. There's no spirit in them, no life at all. What brought ye to a place like this ? '

' We came looking for old churches,' said I.

' Churches ? ' shouted the pig-buyer, handing out another dollop of notes and stuffing the railway voucher in his trousers pocket. ' Churches ? Sure, they have no churches up here, man. There's nothing at all here. Go to Mullingar,' he added, in the tone of one advising me to ' Go west, young man.' ' Go to Athlone ! That's where they have the fine churches ! '

## 27

WE took the pig-buyer's advice and went on to Athlone. In Athenry we struck a really shocking spot, for the castle was being used as the public lavatory of the town, and the Early English priory church as the town ball alley ; and as the balls had a tendency to go through the fine west window, the west window had simply been cemented up.

It was Célimène's turn to go for the key, and she returned after a few minutes with a very long face.

'He says he won't let us in,' she said. 'He wanted money from me.'

'Oh, did he ?' said I, seeing an opportunity for indulging my rancour against that whole disgusting town. 'Show him to me !'

I found the caretaker waiting outside his cottage for us, leaning defiantly against the wall, his arms folded and fight in his eyes.

'Is this the man ?' I asked.

'That's the caretaker,' she said.

'Do you mind letting us have the key of the church ?' I asked as politely as I could.

'I will not give anyone the key,' he shouted. 'Not unless they pay my charges first.'

'Who owns the church ?' I asked.

'I own the church,' he replied truculently.

'You own it ?' said I.

'Yes, I own it, I own it, and no one goes inside that gate without paying my charges first.'

'Isn't that church a National Monument in charge of the Board of Works ?' I asked.

'No,' he said. 'It is my property.'

'The police will soon tell us that,' said I, and cycled off to the barrack. I didn't know who did own the church, but I had a strong suspicion that it wasn't the man we had been speaking to. The police weren't quite certain either, but they did know that an architect from the Board of Works had recently visited the place, and that was enough for me.

But the gesture was wasted. The mere mention of the police was enough, and by the time I returned the caretaker was quite ready to pay Célimène's charges if that silent young woman would only oblige him by looking at the church. He rushed to open the gates for us, and ran frantically about, trying to show us the attractions, while we tried to avoid him. ' Come here, can't ye, come here and look at this ! ' he cried to us from in front of some tomb, and we had to pretend we were not interested in it. I defy anyone with a sense of humour to see architecture like that. Anyhow, the place was in a shocking state. (In reply to my formal complaint, the Board of Works informed me that the caretaker had been reprimanded, but that in the view of the Commissioners the cementing-up of the west window did not affect the stability of the building ! What was it Joyce called us ? A race of clodhoppers ?)

Now, as to Athlone, I am afraid we should never have seen the pig-buyer's church but that it happened to rain precisely as we were passing it. It was a very expensive-looking building, for it had pale-green pillars of Connemara marble, and altar rails of pink French marble, and a pulpit of yellow Siennese marble ; an altar to the saints of Ireland with a picture of St. Patrick on the Reek and four Connemara marble candlesticks in the form of Irish round towers, all simultaneously damaged by lightning ; and as well as these, four shrines with four groups of life-size statuary, including a Pietà after Michelangelo, and one of the well-known Biblical story of David singing before Moses — Michelangelo's Moses !

We set out, pushing our bikes into the teeth of a gale, sheltering from squalls behind hedges and barns, on a desolate road which the map-makers said was in Leinster, though any fool could see it was in Connacht, with boglands to right and left of it, black pine-cones of turf against mother-of-pearl skies and the bright blue hills over by the Shannon Gap for which we were making. The cottages were dirty and unkempt, and we followed a tall, indolent man in shirt-sleeves, with his hands in his trousers pockets, who dexterously guided a frightened cow with well-placed kicks in the throat and belly — an inspiring sight. We hadn't gone far before I had to mend my first puncture.

By the time the Chinese-green screen of flat hillocks that stood between us and the river had opened up and we saw the belfry of Clonmacnois in the distance, I was exhausted. Célimène cycled on to find us a bed for the night. She had the misfortune to make her enquiries of an old gentleman who gave her a lecture on Irish history instead. Of course, with her English accent and appearance, she was God's gift to an oppressed Gael.

' You didn't happen to listen in last night ? ' he asked.

' No,' she said wearily. ' Why ? '

' There was a broadcast about Clonmacnois.'

' Oh,' she asked, ' was it good ? ' (That was the English blood breaking out in her. Why didn't she say that she had written it ?)

' Wonderful ! ' he said enthusiastically. ' The whole history of Clonmacnois from the earliest times.'

' But what I really want to know is whether we can get lodgings somewhere for the night,' she persisted.

' No, lady,' he said firmly. ' There is no hotel accommodation in Clonmacnois since the English burned the abbey guest-house in 1552. You should take a good look at the ruins.'

' We won't be able to look at much if we have to walk to Ballinasloe for a hotel,' she said, ignoring this palpable hit.

' Oh, there's no need to do that,' he said. ' There's a good hotel at Shannonbridge.'

' You're sure of that ? ' she asked eagerly.

' Oh, certain. I know a man that stops there.'

' And you think they'll have a room ? '

' They're bound to at this time of year. Have a look at the ruins. They're well worth it.'

' We will,' she was saying meekly as I rode up, exhausted.

' There's a chapel that was built by Queen Darvorgilla,' he said.

There are certain occasions when any reference to Irish history sends the blood to my head.

' Is there a place we can stay ? ' I asked angrily.

' Not since the year 1552,' he repeated, giving Célimène a look to see if she was repenting the doings of her ancestors, ' when the English from Athlone burned the guest-house of the monastery.'

' Come away,' I said, turning my back on him.

' I'm afraid it's going to rain again,' said Célimène, still hoping to rouse compassion in him.

' Oh, not at all, not at all,' he said with a good glance round the sky. ' The rain is over for the day. Have a look at the chapel. Queen Darvorgilla built it before she wrote " The Valley lay Smiling before Me ".' (This was his coy way of referring to Darvorgilla's affair with Diarmuid ; anyway she didn't.)

' Come on, for God's sake ! ' I said, feeling like murder.

' When the English were still barbarians,' he shouted after us, ' the great Alcuin was studying here under Professor Colgan.'

' Jaysus ! ' said I. I think it was the reference to Colgu as ' Professor Colgan ' that finally got me down.

' Cheer up ! ' said Célimène, going all girl-guidish. ' He said we'd have no more rain.'

' He said Alcuin studied at Clonmacnois,' I snarled.

' Maybe he knows something about rain,' said Céliméne.

' A man like that wouldn't know about anything,' said I.

' Anyway, we can change our clothes and get a decent meal at Shannonbridge,' said she.

' I don't believe there's any hotel at Shannonbridge,' I said sourly. (My prophetic soul !)

Like the pair of imbeciles we were, we left our English-made bicycles outside the graveyard wall in order to save ourselves the labour of carrying them over the stile, and the decent woman who sells the guides took pity on us, and lit a smoky turf fire in her sitting-room for us while Célimène made the tea.

It wasn't enough to cheer us. There are more cheerful spots in the world than Clonmacnois, and pleasanter ways of seeing them than in wet clothes on a showery evening. It was nothing but a dirty graveyard on a slope above the river ; a sea of foundered crosses, gravestones and nettles round a tightly-packed village of ruined chapels, cold-grey with a leprous mottling of flake white, and sharp gables that wounded the sky. By the graveyard wall was a great grey stump of a round tower, and near the river-bank a smaller tower and a ruined Romanesque chancel. The Protestant church, a decent little bit of work, was one of the chapels restored, and the Catholic one a wooden shed, with a wire front so that the statues inside couldn't break out. In the so-called cathedral there was the remains of a Romanesque door, and a goodish fifteenth-century moulded door with very bad figure sculpture, and in one of the chapels a pleasant thirteenth-century window, not unlike the same sort of work at Inishmain.

Darvorgilla's chapel of the nuns lay up the river-bank, but nothing much remained of it except two little semicircles of rosy sandstone with a doorway in one and a chancel arch in the other, their beautiful, irrelevant Romanesque carving half washed away by wind and rain. The official guide-book which we had bought made us gnash our teeth. On the official assumption that adultery is a form of angina pectoris it referred to Darvorgilla as ' the unhappy queen ' and ' the ill-fated queen ', and tactfully suggested that she had probably built the nuns' church as penance for her affair with Diarmuid MacMurrough — a race of clodhoppers !

It was a desolate hole, though it probably looked its best on a rainy evening like that from the river-bank, when the light stole suddenly out from behind walls of weeping cloud and streaked the wide bow of the river with its miles and miles of brown and tile-green flats through which a canal barge nosed in silence, the only sign of life. The blue Connacht hills were low on the horizon, and the slope of the graveyard, with its ruined gables and round tower, was silhouetted against a dazzling cascade of silver light.

But then the light went out, and the wind sprang up, and before we had gone a mile I knew exactly why the English had burned Clonmacnois, for Célimène's back tyre had been deliberately punctured in a hundred places. We walked the rest of the way, and it poured, as I had known it would, and, of course, there wasn't a hotel at Shannonbridge and hadn't been one for many a year.

Even the two Civic Guards who took us in and coddled us, failed to find us a bed in the village. They did everything else for us, bless them! They put us before a roaring fire in the day-room, made us tea, went out and knocked up the man in the shop to get a new tube for us, and put it in themselves. Célimène by this time was shameless. There is a stage of exhaustion at which even the best of women lose all modesty, and she was eyeing a bedstead and mattress in a corner of the room.

When we set out again, about eight, we found that her back axle was broken. Whether this was also revenge for the burning of Clonmacnois I do not know, but the Guards went off a second time, returned with a new axle, and started to take the bicycle asunder. Every few minutes there was a knock, and they challenged the newcomer, who proved to be another member of the Local Defence Force, bringing in the wind and rain with him and invariably greeting the Guards with ' That's a shocking night ! ' It was their drill night, but they didn't do any drill, for all were roped into the repair of the bicycle.

It was after midnight and still blowing and pouring when we set out across the last eight miles of bog to Ballinasloe. We hadn't gone a mile when the rain came down in torrents. With my spectacles wet, I could see nothing at all, and had two bad falls. We walked on till we came to a farm-house, but when we knocked them up they wouldn't let us take shelter — they probably thought we had come down by parachute. We tried another house, but they didn't reply at all. We were whinging with misery when the bicycle lamps revealed a farmyard gate and beyond it a tin-roofed shed with a country cart in it.

It had no doors, but it had its back to the wind, and we found plenty of straw in the cart. We took off our wet clothes, covered ourselves with such dry things as we had in our knapsacks, and then packed ourselves into the cart, out of the way of rats. It was very short; we had to keep our knees well bent, and every time we tried to turn in the bed the shafts reared off the ground. You couldn't make love in a cart like that unless you did it standing on your head. We lay there, propped up on the steep slope of the shafts, looking mournfully out at the black and raging night. The rain battered off the corrugated-iron roof; the cattle stirred uneasily next door, and odd cars and cyclists coming out of Shannonbridge lit up the eddying columns of rain and the haystack in the yard.

Towards dawn the wind shifted and turned to a gale. We heard voices and then saw lantern-light coming from the direction of the gate and shining faintly up into the roof. We thought it must be troops searching for the parachutists, and prepared ourselves for a walk back to Shannonbridge in the rain, but instead it turned out to be men from the farm-house across the road, making the haystack fast. They looked fine and wild with their enormous shadows under the black cliff of the haystack, reminding me of some scene from a novel of Hardy's, but I was in no humour for the merely picturesque. I had no fancy for explaining to an incredulous countryman what I was doing with a woman in his cart at that hour of the morning, even though you couldn't make love in it. He had probably never tried.

We held hands and didn't even whisper, but our luck seemed to be dead out. The man with the lantern ambled over towards the shed and playfully turned the light on our two bicycles. Then he stood there transfixed, and probably a great deal more frightened than we were.

'It's all right,' I shouted. 'We got caught in the rain and came in here for shelter.'

'All right, sir,' he said, after a moment's stupefaction, and then himself and the others moved away. We expected them to return with shot-guns, but they had sense enough to let us alone, and we slept and woke, aching all over. The storm had spent itself and the whole landscape was bright. It was an unforgettable impression. Connacht is so low, so grey, that it is only early morning and late evening with their wide acres of shadow which bring out its scanty modelling ; the quarry, the dark semicircles of turf, the low whitewashed farm-houses where the horizontal light creeps in the doorways and picks out the black and red of cattle in their byres.

We made our breakfast in the farm-house where a sleepy baby was leaning contemplatively over the edge of the tea-chest which served it for a pen, looking into the fire, and then cycled on into Ballinasloe.

## 28

BALLINASLOE is the terminus of the canal, the last frontier post in the eighteenth-century penetration of the Gaelic Wild West, as you can still see by the houses. The fact does not seem to be appreciated by the inhabitants, who lean towards the Red Indian persuasion. The exterior of the Catholic church was surrounded by groups of statuary representing various incidents in the life of Christ. One, by the east end, showed Him carrying a cross inside a ruined cloister of Ruabon brick. On the other hand the monument in the main street showed that the local stone-cutters, the most conservative of men, are still at the twelfth century and Clonfert.

It was getting on towards evening when we finally reached Clonfert. It lies on the bank of the canal ten miles from any-where in a grazing land of tiny, tree-shadowed, winding roads where all good tinkers go when they die. At a bend in the road, against a dark background of wet trees, framed between small, shadowy, yellow gate-posts and flooded with evening light, was the oddest little church in Ireland ; a cathedral no bigger than a respectable bungalow, with a tapering brown Franciscan tower, which apparently had no means of support, in exactly the wrong position above the west gable, and a little Romanesque doorway, its two jambs leaning on one another's shoulders like two drunks swearing eternal friendship. The door was surmounted by a magnificent pediment which resembled some queer pointed head-dress, draped in folds of arches which flowed downward and outward, every stone carved to the consistency of lace.

It was a cathedral porch in miniature, the Lord's Prayer written on the back of a stamp, or whatever other *tour de force* you fancy, and we should have brought a magnifying glass to study it. I have a theory, not put forward for the serious attention of antiquaries, that the masons, notoriously a restless race of men, first built the little chapel for Darvorgilla at Clonmacnois, but found the site too draughty and the natives too vindictive ; and when at last they reached this paradise of tinkers, decided to settle down and bring up their families. That required that the work should be lingered out, so on the jambs and archstones they lavished every pattern they knew, and, when these gave out, they simply invented new ones. And there they worked contentedly under the shade of the trees while their babies grew into fat little putti who stole their tools and did odd jobs of carving on their own, till the steward fretfully complained of the expense.

'Arrah, your holiness,' cried the masons, 'what signifies a month or two more or less ? There won't be a church in Ireland like it when 'tis done.' Nor is there. The limestone order about the door (inferior to the original work which has been built into the inner wall) was the belated inspiration of the fifteenth-century mason who added chancel arch and tower, and it says a lot for the doorway that his dumpy, candid saints and angels scarcely disturb its tranquil gaiety. Nor does the tower, though, for all its tapering Franciscan effeminacy, it is far too heavy for the tenth-century front. It has an air of the most intense decorum ; if both came alive you know that the tower would go to tea with the rector while the porch got itself run in for being drunk and disorderly.

At this point, being (except when roused) the most modest man alive, I would have gone away without seeing the interior, but Célimène insisted on going for the key. I argued with her, pointing out that the guide-book only said the east window was 'good', and that if you deducted 'good' from 'charming', which was what it said of Ross Errily, there was very little left. The woman was in an obstinate mood and we got the key.

As usual she was right, for the interior, restored though not unduly, was just as quaint and lovely as the front ; the tall slender arches that support the tower from inside the porch ;

the eighth-century tombstone built into the wall (elsewhere they throw them into sheds); the pointed chancel arch with another little round-headed arch thrown in for the fun of it, and decorated (by the mason who revised the door) in the most inconsequent manner with the usual fifteenth-century faleals — angels, mermaids, fish and sea-serpents.

Above all there was the east window. It is usually supposed to be earlier than the door; the authorities say eleventh century, the guide-book said twelfth, but it looked to me like thirteenth-century Transitional work of the same kind as the fine window in Hynes' Chapel in Kilmacduagh. It consists of two narrow, round-headed shafts of light set far apart in panelled splays which spread across the full width of the chancel as it were on the open pages of a book. It is a most brilliant and daring bit of work, and it certainly took our breath away. The door-way was sheer virtuosity but this was a work of art. Even that old stick Brash, whom I consulted later, was shaken out of his usual antiquarian torpor by it, for he breaks out into panegyric: ' The design of this window is chaste and beautiful, the mouldings simple and effective, and the workmanship superior to anything I have seen either of ancient or modern times '.

That, extravagant as it seems, was exactly how we felt. For the first time we felt that we had really seen enough. We got hot water from a cottage down the road and had supper on the edge of the canal under the wide enveloping wing of a draughty horseshoe bridge, listening to the chugging of a barge on its way up to Ballinasloe, and watching the swallows flick circles of shadow in the reed-hatched canal that stretched in a straight line between us and the hills over the Shannon Gap through which we were bound.

In the late evening we went on, blowing kisses to the little old church, which for all I know may have returned them. I think it liked us. Again the syrupy calm of that flat green country enveloped and smothered us; the Tudor chimney-pots of a fortified house rose dark above the roadside, and beyond it under a hedge was the orange glow of a tinker's fire. Around it sprawled a family who might have been the ghosts of good tinkers who had never disgraced themselves by marriage in church, and now enjoyed the peace of the eternal camp-fire in the shady lanes behind Ballinasloe.

## 29

THE rest of that day is almost a blank in my mind except for a vague impression of Eyrecourt in the dusk and a fine house with 'hanging gardens' by the road, and an intelligent-looking man telling us they had just uncovered a ceiling showing St. Patrick and the snakes. The Big House had been gutted and the staircase bought by an American. 'Four thousand pounds he paid for it. The finest staircase you ever saw. You could drive a two-ton lorry up and down and across the landing.'

Then the glory of the day went out ; the rain began to fall quietly and steadily, and by the time we reached Portumna we were drenched. We walked up and down a dark street of low Georgian houses, misdoubting what was in store for us. Célimène solved the problem as usual by throwing herself on the mercy of the Civic Guards ; since Shannonbridge she had developed a tendency to look on every policeman as her big brother. Sure enough, the big brothers got us put up in a very nice little lodging-house, and nothing troubled us again till we were waked round about dawn by the noise of carts and cattle. 'Fair day,' said I, and fell asleep again.

When I woke for the second time the sun was shining, and to my astonishment when I went to the window, I saw masses of geraniums and flowers in window-boxes along the whole length of the street. They looked enchanting, and for a while I felt that there must be a catch in it somewhere. But it was just the same downstairs. Through the shop window of the room where we had breakfast we saw an absolutely spotless main street with shrubs outside every house and shop. Some were on expensive mahogany stands, others in butter-boxes painted bright red or green, and they transformed the decent, common-place street till you felt you had gone to sleep and woken up in an entirely different country — probably Holland. When a flaxen-haired girl came out with a feather duster and dusted her butter-box, I really felt I was going mad.

But the landlady seemed to imply that there was nothing in the least unusual about it. The people of Portumna liked flowers, that was all there was in it. I may be a little credulous on the subject of ghosts ; even my views on the fairies would probably not appeal to the Rationalist Press, but you can't take me in about an Irish country town. I told Célimène there must be a priest behind it, somebody like Father O'Flynn who had a wonderful way with him, and we found out later that there was. It seemed to me a pity they didn't make him a cardinal while they were about it. He would be sure of two converts at any rate.

All the way out of town it was the same ; new white council houses with masses of shrubs and flowers above the porches and whitewashed cottages with gay little window-boxes — the oddest, prettiest, most inspiring thing we met with on all our travels. Then the road turned south, skirting the bog, and for miles we passed a procession of orange-and-blue carts moving out of the town. It was a sunshiny, blue-and-silver morning, and at every side were dandelions, wild daisies and purple clover ; burned furze with its ash-blue colour ; young beech trees caught in the blaze and withered to copper and gold ; dark turf-stacks ; and ahead of us the dark-blue mountains of the Shannon Gap with the bubbling soapsuds of clouds above them.

At Oghilly we caught our first glimpse of the lake with its narrow horizontal strips of island, the deeper water honeycombed with sunlight and flickering slowly and rhythmically like a dance of midges. We boiled our kettle in a field at Mount Shannon. The blue lake was at its foot, and the golden belfry of Holy Island rising out of it. We were as happy as Larry there, sitting under a bush by the wall and shielding our stove from the gusts of wind, till the rain came on in torrents and drove us to shelter again.

I don't know what there is about Holy Island that makes it so mysterious and beautiful from the mainland ; perhaps for me it is some thought of its lights shining in the water for Brian

Boru's galleys moving up the Shannon into Connacht, or quenched before some thunderbolt of the O'Connor's, for this was the channel for raid and counter-raid during all the wars of the little kingdoms. Brian himself built the church, but in the twelfth century the monks added a decorated doorway and a chancel by the Master of the Aghadoe Doorway, which make it just worth the little trip by boat.

Then we cycled on into Tomgraney, an embittered-looking Clare hamlet with a hump of rock in the middle of it and an oak tree growing from the top to commemorate a speech by O'Connell. More important to us, Scawen Blunt addressed another meeting from the same spot. Beside the stumpeen of a castle, and facing a gateway with battlemented walls fully two and a half feet high, was a little sandstone church perched on a hillock. The east end which rose above the road had traces of a couple of lancets and thirteenth-century coign-shafts which gave it a certain classic air. I enquired at the post-office for the key and was told it was lost.

Célimène and I had words on the strength of it. We were both getting tired and cross, and I felt I was misunderstood.

'But it's a tenth-century church,' persisted Célimène. 'The guide-book says it.'

'The guide-book says nothing about the inside,' I snapped.

'The guide-book didn't say much about the east window of Clonfert either,' she replied, being full of spiritual pride about that.

'Oh, very well,' I said, and went back to the post-office.

'Are you quite sure there's no way of getting in?' I asked. 'Isn't the church still used?'

'Only once a fortnight,' said the post-mistress sweetly. 'You see, there are so few of us.'

'But what will you do when the next service becomes due?' I asked.

'Oh, I suppose we'll send for a carpenter,' she said lightly.

'Can't we get through a window?' I asked coldly. (I don't seem to have visualised very clearly the measurements of a tenth-century window.)

'I'm afraid not,' said the post-mistress, either beginning to relent or fearing that she was up against a desperate character who would stop at nothing to get inside. 'You might try our back-door key.'

So I took the back-door key, which would have been very useful in a scrap, and at the sight of it Célimène gave a contemptuous little sniff, as much as to say that but for her . . . I choked down my rage as well as I could to concentrate on the church. The tenth-century front with its massive side pilasters, its cyclopean stones, its doorway tapering to the ponderous lintel, had an Egyptian air that was mightily impressive, though it had lost the high gable which would have given it grace as well, and had a hideous little bell-cote tacked on instead. Bowing my head in the deep and narrow doorway, I remembered with a childish thrill that Brian Boru must have done the same a thousand years before on his way up the Shannon, for he was only a boy when Tomgraney was built, and he gave the monks a belfry like that on Holy Island, which has now disappeared.

The opening of the door knocked all the romance out of it, because his little church had been turned into a whitewashed vestibule, partitioned off into a vestry and a cleaner's room, with an underground heating arrangement in the manner of H. M. Bateman. A door in a modern wall led from it into the twelfth- or more likely thirteenth-century chancel, now a shabby little church like a meeting-house in a back lane. It had a nice little dado, and some kind antiquarian had removed the unsightly lancets and compiled a sort of Romanesque window out of the bits and pieces that were knocking round. There were quite a lot of them, including the remains of two round-headed Transitional windows on the south side, and the rain had pierced the walls and covered the carved stones of one in mildew.

But as usual, Célimène was right, and she knew it, and she stood in silence before the window in the north wall as though she had just given birth to it. It was of Late Romanesque or Transitional type with its chevrons carved in pretty little patterns of birds and flowers. Where the chevrons followed the columns they were flattened at the base, but as they reached the capitals they suddenly became pointed and swept out over the top of the window to form a hood. It was a striking effect, as if sunrays were searching upwards into the roof. Perhaps that was un-intentional, for to people as ignorant of building as ourselves the whole church was a puzzle. The window looked as if it had been made for another wall; the splay did not continue to the exterior so that the ornament was never fully lighted, and the stones at the shoulder had been savaged as if some botching mason had tried to set out the splay and given it up as a bad job; then for the other windows contenting himself with putting up the archstones, using bits of moulding from something else — Célimène suggested the belfry door — for the columns, and even making a mess of these.

Célimène sat down before her window with her legs crossed and began to suck an orange, and when I reproved her she said that was how *she* felt about the Church of Ireland. Then we set out again and I remembered that I had left the camera behind, and she gave me a frozen stare. The fact is, she was chockful of spiritual pride, a weakness that fills me with fury, and all the way along the grand road by the lake we snapped at one another.

' I want buns,' she said when we got to Killaloe, and left me to inspect the cathedral alone while she visited the Italian Ware-house. It was a nice, sleepy, hilly little town. Behind the handsome pillars of an eighteenth-century gateway was a little twelfth-century chapel with a flagged roof, and an Early English cathedral with a low tower, moulded corner buttresses and narrow slits for lancets; but chapel and roof and gate and cathedral were all contemporary in the warm, yellow Killaloe sandstone.

Inside the door was the doorway of the twelfth-century cathedral, something in the manner of the Tomgraney window, but even more brilliant. Danish influence, coming up the river, may account for some of its barbaric richness. A whirligig of ornament flowed up the columns, biting out great segments like slices of orange, rioting in human heads and weird animal shapes, and earthing itself in serpents, rats, wolves and what not. It was splendid stone-cutting, but I found myself thinking of the chilly English doorway in Graiguenamanagh and sighing. It might be the climacteric of Irish imagination when fantasy breaks loose from brains, and everything is thrown pell-mell into decoration ; when we cease to be able to halt ourselves and go on elaborating until no functional basis remains — the point Joyce reached in *Ulysses*, phenomenal in craftsmanship, the interior poverty beginning to show.

From that point of view I preferred the cathedral, though it takes some getting used to. It has been spoiled by the cutting-off of the transepts and the closing of the view half-way down by an impossible glass screen reaching to the roof. Apart from that it has suffered remarkably little from restorers. Thanks to the defensive scale of the lancets, the interior is as black as the hob of hell, but if you can find the switches, the lighting of the chancel is first rate. Unfortunately it doesn't give you much chance of studying the corbels, one of which suggests The Master of the Kilfenora Window, but it does show you what the builder intended in the east window ; a frame that fills practically the whole wall, with a fine ornamented hood. There are scores of churches like this through the west of Ireland, and you may find yourself regretting that they are in ruins and likely to remain so.

We had our tea on the river-bank under the cathedral wall. We made peace. We recognised that in all the articles in dispute, what really ailed us was too much scenery. ' Scenery ? ' said a Belfast man to us in the middle of Connemara. ' Ah'm sick of scenery ! ' Nature, as I say, is all very well in its own way, but it produces a ravenous appetite for civilisation, and Killaloe, after all, was only thirteen or fourteen miles from Limerick. You could nearly smell it up the Shannon ; the Georgian architecture, the lights, the hotels, the pubs, the picture-houses and the resiners in Géronte's. How long was it since we had seen Géronte last ?

At O'Briensbridge, with its tiny sandstone tower lost under

the airy blue side of Keeper, the big clouds, lit with gold, sailed massively up the river like granite boulders and tossed silver streamers of light into the fields and the canal. Away to our right were the long hills down which Octave and his companions had galloped in the family coach. We sang. We passed Georgian mansions, orchards and nursery gardens, and at last we came in the dusk to the familiar bridge guarded by its grey drum towers, and above it the skinny old cathedral tower stood up against the sky, bleak and blue-grey and all old-maidish in its curling papers of battlements. As we cycled by it Célimène suddenly jumped off her bicycle and shouted to me to stop. She stood before a hoarding with her eyes popping out.

'What is it?' I cried in alarm.

'Don't you see?' she cried in a frenzy of excitement.

'No,' I said.

'The poster!'

'What's wrong with the poster?' I asked.

'Her chest, man,' shouted Célimène. 'Can't you look at her chest!'

And there it was, with another poster beside it that said 'Every Poster Tells Its Story'—the picture of the Icilma lass, with a modesty vest of brown paper pasted across her pretty chest!

'Civilisation?' I thought, going cold all over. 'Did I say civilisation?'

DUBLIN,
*September* 1945.

# THE HOGARTH PRESS

This is a paperback list for today's readers – but it holds to a tradition of adventurous and original publishing set by Leonard and Virginia Woolf when they founded The Hogarth Press in 1917 and started their first paperback series in 1924.

Some of the books are light-hearted, some serious, and include Fiction, Lives and Letters, Travel, Critics, Poetry, History and Hogarth Crime and Gaslight Crime.

A list of our books already published, together with some of our forthcoming titles, follows. If you would like more information about Hogarth Press books, write to us for a catalogue:

30 Bedford Square, London WC1B 3RP

*Please send a large stamped addressed envelope*

## HOGARTH LIVES AND LETTERS

*The Journal of a Disappointed Man & A Last Diary* by
W.N.P. Barbellion
New Introduction by Deborah Singmaster

*Samuel Johnson* by Walter Jackson Bate

*As We Were* by E.F. Benson
New Introduction by T.J. Binyon

*Notebooks* of Samuel Butler
New Introduction by P.N. Furbank

*Still Life: Sketches from a Tunbridge Wells Childhood* by
Richard Cobb

*Among Friends* by M.F.K. Fisher

*Musical Chairs* by Cecil Gray
New Afterword by Pauline Gray

*Ivor Gurney: War Letters*
Edited and Introduced by R.K.R. Thornton

*Liber Amoris* by William Hazlitt
New Introduction by Michael Neve

*Gift From the Sea* by Anne Morrow Lindbergh
Afterword by the Author

*Being Geniuses Together 1920–1930* by Robert McAlmon &
Kay Boyle
New Afterword by Kay Boyle

*Humping My Bluey* by Graham McInnes
New Introduction by Barry Humphries
*The Road to Gundagai* by Graham McInnes
New Introduction by Robertson Davies

*A Dominie's Log: The Story of a Scottish Teacher* by A.S. Neill
New Introduction by Hugh MacKenzie

# HOGARTH TRAVEL

## M. F. K. Fisher
### *Two Towns in Provence*

Over the years, M. F. K. Fisher, widely regarded as one of America's finest contemporary writers and most highly esteemed of all authorities on the pleasures of the table, has spent much of her time living and travelling round France. Here she celebrates, in her uniquely perceptive, evocative fashion, Aix-en-Provence and Marseilles. Weaving together topography, history, folklore and personal memoirs with the look, the sound, the smell and (above all, perhaps) the taste of her chosen cities, M. F. K. Fisher provides the traveller, the gourmet and the lover of France and fine writing with unforgettable portraits of two remarkable and highly individual towns.

# Michael Wharton
## *The Missing Will*

'Not to be missed' – *Sunday Times*

Michael Wharton – 'Peter Simple' of the *Daily Telegraph* – has for years been writing the most consistently funny and perceptive of newspaper columns, described by Kingsley Amis as 'a treasure house of truth, fantasy and wit'. The same can be said of this masterly slice of autobiography. From early life in Bradford, through a lamentable career at Oxford, army service in India and debauched years in post-war Bohemia to his desk in London, Michael Wharton hilariously charts the making of a remarkable satirist and a 'state-registered melancholiac'. 'Everyone should read his book who wants to know how an intelligent and civilised man can survive in the modern world.' (*Auberon Waugh*)

# Richard Cobb

## *Still Life*

### Sketches from a Tunbridge Wells Childhood

*Still Life* is a classic memoir. In it, Richard Cobb takes us through the streets and houses of his childhood – down Poona Road, along by the Grove Bowling Club, and on past the taxidermist's and 'Love, Fruit and Vegetables' shop – recapturing, with the innocence of a lonely boy, the snobberies and eccentricities of secure middle-class England in the Twenties and Thirties.

'strange and wonderful' – Hilary Spurling, *Observer*

'a rare treasure' – John Carey, *The Sunday Times*

Robert Louis Stevenson
*The Amateur Emigrant*
New Introduction by Jonathan Raban

In 1879 Fanny Osbourne telegraphed Robert Louis Stevenson in Edinburgh, begging him to join her in California. First published in 1895, this is Stevenson's traveller's notebook, a shrewd and sympathetic record not only of the people and places encountered en route but also of his spiritual journey of self-discovery. *The Amateur Emigrant* is the best account ever written of *the* great adventure of the nineteenth century, the passage to the New World.

'The best book he ever wrote – a marvellous piece of writing. . .' – *Jonathan Raban*